thumped

Sch

Also by Megan McCafferty:

bumped

www.meganmccafferty.com

thumped

MEGAN McCAFFERTY

CORGI BOOKS

THUMPED
A CORGI BOOK 978 0 552 56622 3

First published in Great Britain by Corgi,
an imprint of Random House Children's Books
A Random House Group Company

This edition published 2012

1 3 5 7 9 10 8 6 4 2

The Random House Group Limited supports the Forest Stewardship Council (FSC®),
the leading international forest certification organization. Our books carrying the FSC
label are printed on FSC®-certified paper. FSC is the only forest certification scheme
endorsed by the leading environmental organizations, including Greenpeace. Our paper
procurement policy can be found at www.randomhouse.co.uk/environment.

MIX
Paper from
responsible sources
FSC® C016897

Set in Bembo

Corgi Books are published by Random House Children's Books,
61–63 Uxbridge Road, London W5 5SA

www.**kidsatrandomhouse**.co.uk
www.**randomhouse**.co.uk
www.**totallyrandombooks**.co.uk

Addresses for companies within The Random House Group Limited can be found at:
www.**randomhouse.co.uk/offices**.htm

THE RANDOM HOUSE GROUP Limited Reg. No. 954009

A CIP catalogue record for this book is available from the British Library.

Printed and bound in Great Britain by CPI Group (UK) Ltd, Croydon, CR0 4YY

For everyone who helped me celebrate
the Summer of Yes.

FIRST

"What good is it for someone to gain the whole world, yet forfeit a soul?"

—Mark 8:36

harmony

melody

I FACE MY REFLECTION, AN ENGORGED DISTORTION I BARELY recognize anymore.

"I'll do it this time," I say to the mirror.

I mean it too. I'm alone here in my bedroom. The blades are sharp enough and there's no one here to stop me but myself.

Until they come for me.

"Harmony!" Ma calls from down the hall. "You're missing your own nesting party!"

My housesisters and I have been preparing for this party for eight and a half months. Every morning I've joined Katie, Emily, and Laura in their household for prayer and purposefulness. Now we're stocking the nursery's shelves with the cloth diapers, knitted booties, and cotton jumpers we have to show for our collective efforts.

All four of us received the sacrament of marriage on the same day in a group ceremony. We're all with child, but I'm the furthest along and the only one carrying twins. I'm also three years older than they are, so that often makes me feel more like a housemother than a housesister to them. For these reasons, they say, the Church Council voted to give Ram and me our own house to keep, the only couple in the settlement that doesn't have to share with three other families.

There's a gentle knock on the door as it opens. I quickly conceal the shears in my apron pocket.

"May I come in?" Ma asks as she pokes her head in the room. "Are you still woozy?"

I'd felt fine all morning until Ma had presented me with two exquisite hand-stitched quilts in the traditional pattern of interlocking hearts and halos.

"May you be as blessed as I have been," Ma had said as she handed over her gift, a gesture that symbolized the bestowment of motherhood—of womanhood—from one generation to the next.

At that moment, I had to leave the nursery. I couldn't breathe in that room. It felt like four tiny feet were stomping my windpipe when in fact the twins hadn't moved inside me at all.

Now Ma reaches up to press her palm against my sweaty forehead. Without thinking, I clutch my hand against hers and am somewhat surprised by how cool her skin feels under mine. She inhales sharply, so I know that she's startled by the gesture too. I'm relieved when she doesn't resist because I can count on our two joined hands how many times in my sixteen-almost-seventeen years we've had a moment alone together like this. Our household never had fewer than a dozen children at one time to care for, so Ma always had to be efficient with her time and attention. Ma is raising eight of the neediest children in the settlement right now, all of whom are under the age of five. Surely there are infants crying in their bassinets, waiting to be soothed. Babies she didn't give birth to—like me—but were placed by the Church Council to be raised by her righteous example.

When she retracts her hand, mine falls away and hangs limply at my side.

"Would it help to know that I felt overwhelmed during my first pregnancy?" she asks. "I wasn't that much older than you are now."

Before the Virus, women could wait until they turned eighteen to get married and have babies. Now, for all but a very few of us around the world, within a year or two of that birthday marks the end of our child-bearing years. At sixteen-almost-seventeen, I'm considered a very late bloomer.

"Put all your faith in God. He will never give you anything more than you can handle."

Ma stands up and brushes the invisible dust off her apron as if the matter of my overwhelming maternity is all settled. She is nothing if not practical. When your whole life has been devoted to taking care of others, you have to be. Small and stout with curly black hair and brown eyes, Ma has never looked anything like me. But for some reason those physical differences are all I can see right now.

"Take a few moments to pray on it before rejoining us." She smiles benignly, then slips out the door.

Ma means well. She always does. But I feel like I've already been dealt more than I can handle. I've seen that formerly empty room for what it was destined to be all along: a nursery. Two quartersawn oak cribs, one against each wall. A changing table stacked with cloth diapers. A braided rug on the floor in soft shades of yellow and green. A glider and ottoman near the window. But try as I might, I can't envision the babies sleeping in their cribs. Being changed out of a soiled diaper. Or rolling happily on the rug. And it is all but impossible to picture myself rocking back in forth in the glider, nursing a ravenous baby on each breast. I know now, beyond a shadow of a doubt, that unlike the three other girls in the room with Ma, I will never live up to her example.

A riot breaks out in my belly. The thrashing of four tiny feet, the pounding of four tiny fists. The twins are awake.

"Are you two trying to stop me?" I whisper. "Or do you want me to go through with it?"

Another round of kicking and punching.

I choose to interpret this as a sign of encouragement.

After eight and a half months, I'm convinced the twins feel as trapped as I do. I take the shears out of my pocket and return my attention to the mirror with a renewed sense of purpose. I grip the handle, all ready to go through with my plan, when I'm stopped by the sound of my name once more.

"Harmony!"

Only this time, it's not Ma. And it's not coming from down the hall.

"It's me . . ."

It's *him*.

"Please pick up . . ."

Calling to me from the MiVu screen.

Oh my grace. I've blinded his profile countless times, but he keeps coming back.

"Harmony . . ."

I don't want to look at his face. I draw upon every last ounce of strength I have left not to look. . . .

But I can't help myself. And there he is, larger than life on the screen, looking every bit as tortured and handsome as he did the last time he tried to contact me a few weeks ago.

Jondoe. Or *Gabriel*, as he should be known.

No, I will only know him as Jondoe.

"You're at thirty-five weeks today, Harmony. I just want to make sure you're okay. . . ."

He looks so sincere. But how can I ever believe someone who gets paid to lie?

"Please let me see you . . . I miss your face."

Right now I hold all the power. I can see him. But he can't see me.

And if I have my way, he never will.

I briskly walk over to the MiVu screen and blind his profile again.

melody
harmony

MY TWIN IS EVERYWHERE, AND YET SHE'S NOWHERE TO BE seen.

"She blinded me again," Jondoe says with a sigh, a sigh with 180 pounds of perfectly sculpted musculature behind it. Not that his hot body is doing him a bit of good these days. He's miserable, and it's all because of my sister.

"I'm sorry," I say. "But I told you she would."

Harmony is the most determined person I've ever met. Eight and a half months ago, she made up her mind that returning to Goodside to deliver the twins was the "godly" thing to do. She hasn't wavered in that decision, despite all our repeated attempts to woo her back to this side of the gates. Harmony insists on raising them with Ram, even though there's zero chance that her husband is the true father.

"Do you have any idea how hard it is to be here?" Jondoe asks. "Surrounded by girls who look *exactly* like her?"

The irony is, I'm Harmony's identical twin and I'm not even one of the girls Jondoe is referring to. I scan the rowdy crowd from the safety of the one-way window wall of our second-story VIP room. There are a lot of girls who look just like her at a distance. It's impossible to count just how many dyed blondes are dressed in Conception Couture knockoffs of Harmony's green maternity gown.

Jondoe anxiously chews on his thumbnail. "Is it even safe for her to deliver in Goodside? Do they even have real doctors there?"

"Delivering is what they do best," I say, taking Harmony's word for it because that's all I have. I mean, Goodside midwives must know what they're doing if they routinely deliver babies for teen newlyweds, right?

But before I can say anything else to reassure him, my agent, Lib, comes barreling toward us wearing the latest TEAM HOTTIE T-shirt under the pink and blue flashing lumina jacket that has become his iconic trademark. I hate that shirt. I especially hate that I'm wearing the same exact shirt in size XXXL Maternity.

"Your FANS are ready for YOU! Are YOU ready for THEM?"

"We're ready." I look to Jondoe for confirmation, but he's too distracted to pay me or Lib or this party any mind.

Lib has no time for such self-indulgent melodrama,

unless he's the one being self-indulgently melodramatic. He pokes Jondoe in the ribs.

"Ow!" Jondoe says, rubbing the spot.

"You think you can interrupt your VERY IMPOR-TANT LIP POUTING long enough to fulfill your contractual obligations?"

Jondoe shrugs.

Lib shoots me a *he's your problem* look, then takes off to welcome the incoming crowd.

As soon as he's out of earshot, Jondoe leans in.

"I can't believe Harmony is really going to stay there with Ram." His voice is on the verge of breaking. "You promised that she'd come around before she delivered."

"I thought she would . . ."

I really did too.

"You told me this was how I could help her," he says bitterly, more to himself than me. "That's the only reason I'm still here . . ."

He silences himself as the room fills with fan clubbers, contest winners, and corporate muckety-mucks, all eager to have their fotos taken with us.

I believe Jondoe has sincere feelings for my sister. I mean, the guy can sell underwear like nobody's business, but that pretty much pushes the limit of his skills as an actor. There's no way that he could have faked the change I've seen in him for the past eight and a half months. I know it has sucked for Jondoe—I can relate all too well to wanting to be with someone you can't have.

I bring my lips to his ear.

"She's the reason I'm here too," I say. "And there's still time."

But even as I say these words, I know that with each minute that goes by, they are that much closer to becoming more lies.

Our audience swoons over our whispered sweet nothings, the secrets shared by two gorgeous ReProductive Professionals who have done the unheard of:

We have fallen deeply and lustily in love.

At least that's what we need everyone to believe they're seeing.

harmony

melody

I DID IT! IF I CAN RESIST JONDOE, I CAN DO ANYTHING. I'M flush with a rush of energy like I haven't felt since my second trimester.

With one hand I take hold of my long braid and extend it as far as it will go. With the other hand I open the shears. I place the thick golden plait inside the mouth of the scissors, close my eyes, and . . .

"What in Heaven are you *doing*?"

My husband has a knack for showing up precisely when he's not wanted.

Ram is frozen in the door frame, his whole face etched with concern. I know this gentle giant cares about me, loves me even, just not in the way in he should. And yet, I cared enough about him to come back here because he needed me more than I needed him. It's how my ma raised me, after all, to live in JOY:

Jesus first, Others next, Yourself last.

That's the excuse I use anyway, whenever anyone asks why I gave up on my fresh start in Otherside before it even had a chance to begin. Yet, as far as I know, according to stolen conversations I've had with Melody, there's really only *one* person who asks. But after everything that has happened, I don't think I'll ever be convinced that Jondoe needs me out there nearly as much as Melody says he does, and certainly not more than Ram needs me here. Jondoe has amassed a fortune making fools fall for his untruths. We *both* have, actually. But I won't be *his* fool again.

Or anyone else's.

Ram approaches me slowly, carefully, like I'm a rabid dog or something worth fearing.

"Your ma and your housesisters are waiting for you," he says.

His hand is outstretched, hoping I'll willingly give him the scissors without an argument. Praying that I will, against all odds, act like the subservient wife he's never asked me to be. Instead, I take an even tighter grip on the handles, clamp down firmly one . . . two . . . three times until the braid comes away in my fist!

Ram and I take a moment to marvel at it, as if this length of hair were a rare and dangerous creature I had hunted down and caught with my bare hands.

I'm still staring at my quarry when I hear the high-pitched gasps.

"Oh my grace!"

Ma tries in vain to block my housesisters from getting a clear look at what I've just done. Hands flutter to mouths, cheeks, and eyes in disbelief.

"The Orders!" my housesisters cry out in unison. "She broke the Orders!"

I lock eyes with the woman who raised me. There's no comfort to be found in her gaze, only sadness. I hope she knows this isn't her fault. Ma treated all her daughters—by birth and by adoption, before me and after—the same. Forty-seven out of forty-eight of the children she raised were receptive to her teachings of the Word. I don't know why I am the exception.

"I'm praying for you," Ma says as she ushers Katie, Emily, and Laura out of the doorway. There's a finality to the way she says it, as if she's brushing me off like so much invisible dust on her apron.

The front door slams and Ram finally speaks. There's a catch in his voice. He's scared. And I am too.

"What *are* you doing, Harmony? What are *we* going to do?"

At eight and a half months along, I don't have much time left for figuring out the answer. I rub the naked nape of my neck and do what I haven't been able to do since I came back all those months ago: Tell the truth.

"I don't know."

melody

harmony

"COME, EVERYONE," LIB ANNOUNCES. "AND MEET THE HOTTEST half of The Hotties!"

That's me. One half of the Hot Twins Having Twins. When a series of focus groups thumbs-downed that label because it was too wordy for the MiNet, Harmony and I were officially rebranded The Hotties. Marketers find our story irresistible. Identical twin girls separated at birth, raised in drastically different environments, due to deliver sets of twin girls on the same day. This is the wildly antici- pated event known as Double Double Due Date, or D4.

Harmony and I target two different types of consumers. Married to Ram and a devout member of the superstrict Church, Harmony appeals to conservative shoppers who believe the infertility crisis caused by the Virus is no excuse for committing the sin of premarital sex. And my coupling with Jondoe, the most famous ReProductive Professional on the planet, makes me the role model for liberal spenders who support the rights of Surrogettes and think it's empowering for girls to get paid to breed on their behalf. Together, my sister and I are, according to Lib, a "next-generation synergistic multiplatform global marketing phenomenon." And events like this are necessary if we hope to expand the brand right up to the moment Harmony's water breaks.

It doesn't matter if this if my first or fiftieth fan foto-op. The conversations are remarkably the same.

"You're such a positive role model for my daughter," says Quailey's mom as she shoves a willowy, pillow-lipped, raven-haired thirteen-year-old in front of me. Quailey fills out the trademarked copy of my orange and black #15 Princeton Day Academy varsity soccer jersey better than I ever did. And that's saying something.

"*Mommmm*," she whines, reminding me just how young she really is.

"Surrogetting is just starting to catch on in our neck of the woods," Quailey's mom continues. "I've gotten a lot of grief from the other PTO moms, believe you me." She pats the complicated updo that's popular among women her age. "They don't see the big-picture stuff, so they're content to just let their daughters get knocked up by their down-market boyfriends."

Jondoe mutters something unintelligible, which immediately attracts eyeballs because he's been staring sullenly at his feet throughout the meet and greet so far. You'd think his depressed expression would be a turnoff. But his sadness only makes him more mysterious and magnetic than ever . . . if you're into that sort of thing. Quailey finds him unlookawayable and is desperate to know what he just said.

"What was that?" She's bouncing up and down on her toes. "What? *WHAT?*"

I don't know what he said, but I *do* know how unhinged Jondoe is feeling right now, and I'm afraid of what he'll do.

Fortunately, Quailey's mom is all business. "We admire what UGenXX has done for you," she says, searching around the room. "Is your agent taking on any more clients?"

"Mommmm. For serious. You're so neggy. I'm going to terminate with embarrassment."

I cringe. Did I sound that brainwashed before?

"I'll be happy to give you his password," I lie, just so I can end this conversation.

"Fertilicious!" she says. "It's our dream to see Quailey bump with someone as reproaesthetical as you, Jondoe! It's an investment in her future!"

Jondoe blows out his cheeks with an annoyed *pfffffft* and I swear Quailey is about to peak with pleasure.

"That's the worst advice I've ever heard," he says calmly, looking right at Quailey, who looks like she's about to pass out from the attention.

16

Quailey's mom assumes she's misunderstood him. "What did you say?"

"When you bond with someone in a heart and soul sort of way, you *should* be able to bond physically too. It's like, the most beautiful, most profound experience." He closes his eyes and tilts his head to the ceiling, as if he were basking in an invisible sunbeam. "And once you have it, you never want to settle for anything less. Waiting five minutes to be with someone you love can feel like five years! And waiting five years can feel like . . . forever!"

We all freeze. He's waxed all poetic about Harmony to me privately, but never, ever in public. For Jondoe to go manifesto like this is the equivalent to Harmony carving a pentagram into her forehead and declaring her allegiance to Mephistopheles. I think quickly.

"Which is why it was so awesome that we were contracted to bump together!"

Jondoe looks exhausted from his rant. He lowers his head, opens his eyes, looks at me.

"I can't do this anymore."

Then he walks away from us and out of the room.

"Oh my God!" Quailey chirps. "Did you just, like, break up?" Her eyes are already rolling in their sockets so she can spread this gossip on the MiNet.

"Um . . . he's just . . ." How do I explain what just happened here? I'm getting all panicky now, trying to think of something I can say to put a positive spin on this situation when the door opens and I lose all interest in feigning politeness.

"Zen!"

I'm not the only one who has noticed his arrival. Every head turns as he cuts through the crowd.

"Omigod! He's even breedier than Jondoe!" Quailey gushes, clutching her soccer jersey.

I resent her for being able to say what I cannot.

Zen heads straight for me. I'm all ready to vent to him about Jondoe's latest meltdown over Harmony when I realize that I'm just so off-the-spring happy to see him. Jondoe and Harmony are *not* the kept-apart couple I care about right now.

Zen tries to give me a hug, but we can't get any closer than an arm's length from each other.

"It looks like something has come between us," he says wryly.

We both look down at my massive midsection. It's an old joke, one I've always thought was too true to laugh at, but I smile anyway because Zen makes me smile whether I want to or not.

"Not for much longer," I say, more for my sake than his. "Harmony is thirty-five weeks along."

Zen presses his palm to the parabolic curve of my belly. "And you too."

I've been at it for more than eight months now. And yet it's the littlest slips of my tongue that remind me how difficult it will be to see this commitment through to the very end.

"Right," I say, recklessly placing my hand on top of his, out in the open, where Quailey and her mom and anyone else can see us. A current of electricity passes between us, just enough of a jolt to remind me why I need to take my hand away. "Me too."

harmony
melody

RAM IS PARALYZED. MY MOOD SWINGS HAVE BEEN ENTIRELY unpredictable lately and there's no way he could have ever seen this makeover coming.

"Why did you do that?" he whispers.

I take a moment to consider the question.

"I grew that braid my entire life," I reply, turning over the lank rope of hair in my hands. "That's a lot of hair. And it's a lot heavier than you might think it is. I'm already loaded down by these babies. Why do I need any extra weight on me?"

Ram answers slowly. "Because the Orders say so."

"Exactly." I nod. "But *why*? What does that braid have to do with my ability to worship?"

I posed this question to my housesisters during yesterday's

prayershare and they dismissed it, as they have dismissed all the questions I've asked since I came back. These are the kinds of questions that make me a last-pick partner for sharing a hymnal at Sunday service.

Ram scuffs the floorboards with his feet. "I dunno."

"Me neither."

There's so much I don't know.

I pause for a moment before adding, "I'm thinking about dying it black."

"The braid?"

"No." I rub my scalp. "The rest of my hair. If I don't shave it all off entirely."

What am I trying to prove here? Do I want to prove to them all that my heretical hairstyle has no effect on my relationship with God? Or do I want my outward appearance to reflect who I am on the inside?

An outcast.

Ram steadies himself on the doorjamb.

"But you can't change your hair," he says beseechingly.

"Well, I *can* and I *did*," I say, holding up the braid like a prize. And just like that, I can feel the rush of energy leaving me. I'm convinced the highs and lows of pregnancy are doubled when carrying twins.

I wish I could ask my birthmother about that.

"Don't you have to lead a prayerclique on the MiVu tonight?" Ram asks.

"Yes, I do. A fledgling settlement in Ohio."

The Church Council approved me for the MiVu when they saw the surge in interest in the Church after my sister and I made our debut. It's funny that my own housesisters are hesitant to be seen with me, and yet those who don't know me can't get enough of my testimony. I tell them about how much I regret sneaking away to Otherside, how I was overwhelmed by all the sex and sin and came back to Goodside more dedicated than ever to the Church. The biggest sinners have the best redemption stories, after all.

And they don't even get to hear what *really* happened.

The Council closely monitors my activity, though. I'm only approved for thirty minutes of use per week, all for prescheduled virtual meet-ups with prayercliques around the world who have made generous offerings to our settlement for the privilege of doing so. That money has done our community a world of good. Most of it has been put toward the advanced medical care for the neediest infants rejected by Otherside and embraced by Goodsiders like Ma. Because of my profitable, high-profile role in the ministry, dozens of sick or malformed babies have a chance at a better life. I'm saving them the way the Church saved me seventeen years ago. That's worth something, right?

Still, I've been reprimanded several times for using my spare minutes to get in touch with my sister. My punishment? I wasn't allowed to attend morning prayershare with Katie, Emily, and Laura. Ha! How little the Elders knew about me. What a gift it was to get a break from their sidelong glances and surreptitious prayers for my soul.

"I've got my own mission at that party tonight," Ram says, holding up a thick stack of THE CHURCH SAVES, the autographed tracts the Elders have given him to distribute to the crowd. "I'm already supposed to be there. But I don't know if I feel right leaving you like this after what just happened."

As a man, Ram doesn't need special permission to leave Goodside to spread the Word. He can come and go as he pleases, as long as the Elders are convinced he's serving the Church. The only appearances I can make are on the MiVu, and I've made good on all my obligations so far. But tonight I'm feeling like I just can't do it. All that energy from earlier is seeping out of me like a hole in the well. And—oh my grace—the twins are in a winner-takes-all wrestling match for their share of the womb!

Did Melody and I give our birthmother this much discomfort? I hope to ask her in person some day. Being reunited with my birthmother would make all of this worthwhile. For me, the only advantage to our fame is that it's only a matter of time before our birthmother hears of our amazing story and tries to find us. That's the sole reason I've gone along with The Hotties, a label I personally find both prideful and distasteful.

So far it's been one crushing disappointment after another. Greed is a wicked sin, and none of the couples claiming to be our birthparents have passed the YDNA test that proves they're telling the truth. I pray that our birthmother will catch our smiling faces in an advertisement and realize that Melody and I are the twin girls she left behind at the hospital entrance almost seventeen years ago. It's one of only two prayers I make.

And I hope you'll understand why I might want to keep the second prayer between God and me.

melody

I'M DESPERATE FOR ANOTHER MOMENT ALONE WITH ZEN. I know we can't do much, but I'm aching to be near him. As far as I'm concerned, I've fulfilled my commitment to fan clubbers, contest winners, and corporate muckety-mucks. I'm about to suggest we disappear into the private inner sanctum of the VIP room when Lib screams me back to reality.

"WHY ARE YOU HERE? YOU ARE OF NO USE TO ME RIGHT NOW."

"Always a pleasure to see you too, Lib," Zen replies with an impish grin.

Lib is still pissed at Zen for refusing to go pro.

Lib usually has an eye for spotting potential growth spurts, so no one was more surprised than he was when my best friend shot up four inches in as many months. And, well, every other girl at Princeton Day Academy who had once viewed Zen's insufficient verticality as a liability. Not too long ago, Zen couldn't *give* his DNA away. No girl wanted to take a risk by bumping with a guy who was only five foot seven and a half. Now he's constantly fielding offers from amateurs *and* pros. His biggest problem is that he's running out of believable excuses for why he won't seal a deal already.

Zen is shockingly levelheaded about all this newfound attention from the opposite sex. He's always trying to convince me that the girls aren't interested in him, they're interested in me. Or rather, my fame. But he's wrong. He's not giving due credit to his own humpiness. There's an endless supply of girls from every persuasion and perversion trying to get in his pants. Every. Single. Day.

I honestly don't know how much more I can take. I am for seriously *done* with this bump. The doctors say the twins are pretty much out of preemie danger zone now, so I hope they make their debut very soon. Unfortunately, there are too many Baby Stock Market bets ("speculate on due dates and birth weights") riding on the day, hour, minute, and second of D4, so we can't speed things along artificially.

"How about you and me go somewhere for some hot and heavy hand holding?" I joke, trying to mask just how much I miss his touch.

"That sounds really awesome," Zen says, stealing

26

distracted glances behind me. "But . . . um . . . remember when I said it would be a smart idea to keep up appearances by bringing a plus-one?"

I follow his eyes toward the front door, where none other than Ventura Vida is pushing her way past the bodyguards, boobs first.

I feel like I've belly-flopped into an empty swimming pool.

I've put up with a lot over the past eight and a half months, but I'm not sure I can survive thirty seconds of Ventura Vida. It's so unfair. Here I am, weighed down by an extra forty pounds, while she struts around sexier than ever. Ventura made her last delivery a little over four months ago, though you would never know it from appearances. She's somehow even thinner than she was before she bumped, with two prominent D-cup exceptions.

"Plus one?" I snark. "More like plus three."

It's a lame joke and I'm actually a little relieved when Zen doesn't patronize me by laughing at it.

"She's really not as bad as you think she is," he says quickly, his eyes darting back and forth between me and her as she makes her approach. "You two actually have a lot in common. . . ."

"Really? Or as Ventura would say, *'Rilly?'*"

Ventura puts her best assets to good use as she lunges to hug Zen.

"Hey, partner! Long time no facespace!"

He looks at me from over her shoulder and apologizes

with his eyes. The embrace goes on for waaay longer than necessary. I do everything I can to stop myself from calling the bodyguards to forcibly release her grip on Zen's shoulder blades.

Finally, she lets go, steps back, smiles at me sweetly.

"Hey, Mel. Thanks for the VIP pass! It was rilly nice of you."

"Oh, it was nothing." And because I can't stop myself: "*Rilly.*"

Do not be fooled by such pleasantries. Ventura hates me. She may be president of Princeton Day Academy's Pro/Am Pregg Alliance, but I'm the one that all the girls look up to as their reproductive role model. I'm not bragging, but since I became a Hottie, membership in the Alliance has more than tripled. This weighs heavily on my conscience. Zen assures me that their eagerness to follow me now will only work in our favor later on. I hope he's right.

"Mmm. You smell good!" Ventura says to me brightly.

"I . . . what?"

"Melody: The Fragrance. It smells good."

Oh, right. I had totally forgotten which branch of our brand is being exploited—I mean, *expanded*—today. I had sniffed a few samples and signed off on a scent designed to capture the essence of my half of the twinship. *Melody: The Fragrance* smells like Coke '99, a grass-stained soccer ball, and crisp dollar bills. Harmony's perfume got its inspiration from the Song of Solomon and smells like rose of Sharon, honey, and myrrh.

Zen is standing equidistant between us. He's smiling nervously and is uncharacteristically mute. It's weird. And it's wanking me out.

"Did Zen tell you?" Ventura says. "We terminated the competition in our debate today!"

Since teaming up in September, Zen and Ventura are undefeated debate partners. According to the quikiwiki, "Princeton Day Academy has never before produced such a skillfully persuasive, silver-tongued duo."

Now excuse me while I feign a wave of morning sickness.

"No," I say. "He didn't tell me. We had barely had time to say hello before you showed up."

"Guess what the topic was? Just *guess*!"

"Tell me! I can't wait to hear!"

She's not the only one who can play the nicey-nice game.

She clears her throat. "Government should spend fewer taxpayer dollars in promoting professional pregging for profit and spend more money on social programs that would allow amateur preggers to raise their own children *and* stay in school."

I can see Zen going manifesto in agreement. But Ventura? No way. That would go against everything she stands for. She's wearing an I'M PREGG NATION T-shirt, for Darwin's sake!

"What side did you have to argue? Affirmative or negative?"

Zen and Ventura both laugh at my question. Not in a cruel way but in shared amusement, which actually cuts me more deeply.

"Does it matter?" Ventura asks. "A skilled debater always knows how to win both sides of an argument!"

Zen says the same thing. All the time.

Bleep! Bleep! Bleep!

Gah. *Of course* my Maternal Obligation Monitor has to go off right now in front of Ventura. According to legislation that passed right before I pregged, professional Surrogettes are legally required to wear it at all times. MOM gives a warning bleep at the first sign of excess stress.

"Are you okay?" she asks in her most sincere voice. "Are you feeling *anxious*?" She puts delighted emphasis on the last word.

"No!" I snap. "I'm fine. Just a little too much caffeine today, that's all!"

I can tell from the victorious look on Ventura's face that she's not buying the latest of my many lies.

"Speaking of beverages," Zen says, "let's get you something to drink, Ventura."

As he guides Ventura across the room to the bar, I catch Zen gently brushing his fingertips against the small of her back.

Bleeeeeeeeep!

harmony
melody

RAM IS GETTING ANTSY. "ARE YOU SURE I CAN LEAVE YOU tonight?"

"I'll be fine," I insist, before adding, "the Elders will be disappointed if you don't go. There are a lot of souls that could be saved."

I try to say it like *that's* why I want him to go. When the truth is, I just want him to go. Period.

"Are you sure?" he asks.

"I'm sure," I say firmly. "But come here first."

I'm not a rabid dog anymore. He comes right over to me so I can smooth the lapels on his jacket. At first glance it doesn't seem like what he's got on is all that different from the black suits all men in Goodside wear. But on closer examination, the fabric isn't wool sheared from the settlement's own sheep but the finest cashmere imported from halfway around the world. The stitches aren't uneven but altogether invisible. It's a bespoke suit made by the world's finest craftsmen, but it's fashioned after traditional Church attire. The green maternity gown I'm wearing right now was designed by someone named Chanel, who is apparently very famous in Otherside. That's the kind of money we're earning these days. And as long as I continue to tithe more than I keep, and don't go beyond the Goodside gates again, the Church Council is content to let me continue doing the Lord's work in my own unique way.

Like Jondoe.

His parents believed he was chosen by God for important missionary work, that when he spread his seed, he was sowing the seeds of faith. But did *he* really believe that? Melody says Jondoe wants to make amends for hurting me, which is why he agreed to help us out. My sister would never deceive me about such matters. But how can I be sure that *he* isn't lying to *her* too . . . ?

It's his pleading voice I hear in my head right now.

Harmony, please.

And now, try as I might, I can't stop memories of our one night together from entering my mind. Not just my mind, but my heart, my soul, my *flesh.*

"No!" I shut my eyes and shout. *"No!"*

This is the sin I can never confess out loud.

Ram's whole body is tense, his back arched like a cornered cat. I force a smile to put him back at ease.

"You *sure* you're okay?"

I nod vigorously and give Ram a quick once-over. With his ruddy complexion and formidable frame, he comes across as wholesome and just a little bit fearsome in the way that only makes a man more handsome—at least that's how I remember Lib describing him in a pitch for a deal with a soft drink company. And yet I have never, not once, wanted to press any part of my body against any part of Ram's. This arrangement has worked out for us so far. But how much longer can we keep this up? 'Til death do us part?

I release my grip on his coat. "Now you can go."

Part of me wants to add, *And don't come back.* I mean this in the most merciful way possible. I want to release Ram as Ma has released me.

My husband smiles gratefully and turns to leave. Then he stops himself.

"Should I tell Melody about this?"

He points to the braid, which is now lying limply on the matrimonial quilt stitched by my housesisters in a traditional double wedding-ring pattern. My real wedding ring funded my escape to Goodside last spring. Ram has since offered to replace the ring, and I have declined every time. Ma told my curious prayerclique my fingers were too swollen from my blessings for rings. I hate the idea of Ma lying for me, so I can only hope she believed that was the truth.

She won't have to lie for me anymore.

33

"Harmony?" Ram asks, waving his hands to get my attention. "Should I tell Melody or not?"

"As far as I'm concerned, you're free to tell anyone anything you want."

I'm getting impatient with Ram's loyalty in the face of reality. It's only his fidelity to me and fear of the unknown that makes him stick to me like a cocklebur on my hem. He's as ambivalent about raising a family as I am, but he'll do it because I asked him to. And until now, I tried convincing myself that it was the praiseworthy decision.

But is it the right choice for the babies? For Ram?

For me?

But I'm not supposed to think about what's best for me, am I?

I smile at him weakly. It's all I can muster right now.

"Now go. Please."

Ram doesn't wait for me to say it again. He gives me a quick kiss on the top of my head before bounding out the door, down the stairs, and into the air taxi waiting to take him into Otherside.

I'm alone again. But I know it won't be for long.

As I lie down on the bed, I pay no mind to the emancipated braid as it falls off the edge and onto the floor. It's already too late to stop the loose end from unraveling.

melody
harmony

I'M STILL BLEEPING.

Lib comes out of nowhere, grabs my wrist, and shakes it.

"Can't you shut THAT THING up?"

"Oh, that's hilarious coming from the person who adjusted all the settings."

Lib has no idea how much I'd love to shut this thing up. MOM goes off if it detects too much or too little of *anything* that can do harm to my delivery—make that deliver*ies*—in utero. The bracelet comes with a standardized set of upper (sugar, alcohol) and lower (vitamins, cardio-vascular exercise) limits, but almost every Parental Unit makes customizations based on their own belief system. On the upside, the Jaydens are liberal about caffeine— I can drink one can of soda every day without getting bleeped. But I'd happily give up my beloved Coke '99 if they'd be willing to change their neggy opinion on having sex while pregging.

"But if Jondoe and I have already done it, what's the harm in doing it again?" I asked.

"You could misdeliver!" Lib countered.

"But that's a myth!" I protested.

"You of all people shouldn't underestimate Jondoe's penetrative powers," he replied. "It's just not worth the risk."

Lib doesn't want to take *any* chances with me, his most prosperous client. He's been my agent ever since he persuaded me to go pro at thirteen and negotiated all the details of my Conception Contract with the Jaydens. Most RePro Reps have limited themselves to the money earned in the negotiations between Surrogette (me), Sperm (Jondoe), and Parental Unit (the Jaydens). Lib has always THOUGHT BIG, and when we offered him the opportunity to represent both me and Harmony, he didn't flinch. I'll give him full credit for coming up with The Hotties' many revenue streams. He's made us all wealthier than anyone but Lib could ever have imagined. Because when it comes to money, Lib has a limitless imagination.

I'll admit: It hasn't been all bad. The Hotties were the biggest thing to hit the MiNet in a long time, and it was worth all the hassle just to watch Ventura's status suffer by comparison. We were the right brand at the right time, making our MiNet debut right after the nation's most prolific eighteen-year-old, Zorah Harding, sadly announced that the Virus had finally claimed her uterus and she would not be delivering baby number eleven after all. Before we could blink, The Hotties were global. Memers couldn't go viral fast enough with what we were saying, wearing, eating.

And selling. Always selling. Harmony and I have earned more than enough money to buy our independence. But what if Harmony stands her ground and refuses to choose freedom? Zen insists that no matter what happens with Harmony, I am a "movement in the making." When he starts talking like this, I for seriously consider living off the interest of my earnings, partying my ass off, and never making a single positive contribution to society. If that's what I want to do, I can. I've earned the independence to make that choice.

But as I sit here, fat and cranky, watching helplessly as Zen laughs at one of Ventura's jokes, I can't help but ask myself: At what cost?

"WHERE IS HE?" Lib is back and even shoutier than before.

"Where's who?" I ask distractedly, my eyes still trained on Zen and Ventura.

"Who? WHO?! JONDOE! He's gone OFF THE GRID."

Now is probably not a good time to mention that the last time I saw Jondoe he was in the middle of a sexistential crisis.

"Um . . . He's got to be around here somewhere. . . ." I say unconvincingly, looking out the window and down at the crowd below. It doesn't look any different from any of the other parties thrown in our honor. Harmony's fans are swaying and praying. Mine are dancing, drinking, dosing. The groups don't mingle, but they can coexist in the same room without any drama, which was impossible to imagine just eight months ago. We received medals of honor from the National Association for Procreation for "giving common ground to radically different ideodemographics."

"Oh, wait," I say. "Ram's down there!"

Harmony's husband is working his way through the crowd, making it rain religious tracts like dollar bills in a strip club. He's got a huge smile on his face and—ha!—did I just catch him in a fist pump? Of all of us, I must say that he seems to be the one who gets the most genuine enjoyment out of these events. Either he really lives to serve God, or he really loves a party.

"RAM IS NO JONDOE."

And Lib races off again to berate a Team Hottie intern. I've never seen Lib so stressed out. I think I might have seen an actual wrinkle denting his forehead's synthetic skinfeel.

"Hot-TIES! Hot-TIES!" the crowd chants.

I fear that if I don't give them some face time soon, this party will get real ugly, real fast.

"It's getting crazy down there, huh?"

Zen is back by my side. By himself.

38

"Where's Ventura?"

"In the bathroom."

"Probably to confirm that she's peaking," I say, immediately regretting making any reference to the subject of Ventura's overactive ovaries.

Zen's face is stony. "And if she *is* ovulating? What? You think we're gonna bump pretties tonight?"

Bleeeeeeeeeep! Gah. This thing is worse than the polygraph app.

"Sweet Darwin! You *do*! That's why you're bleeping like a lunatic."

"Maybe I got the ninth-month nutsies a little bit early," I say sarcastically.

Zen doesn't say anything. He knows I'm being ridiculous and doesn't want to dignify that with a response. He takes a moment to quietly sip his Dr. Peppermint soda. I've seen him do this to unnerve his competition in debates, which makes the stalling tactic all the more frustrating.

"Melody . . ."

He takes a step toward me, so we're only inches apart. He tilts his face even closer to mine, and I lift my chin to meet his parted lips. . . .

But he doesn't kiss me.

"You know I have to fake interest or it will look suspicious."

I should keep my voice low. But I'm too frustrated— sexually and otherwise—to do so.

"Your fake interest in her is more convincing than

your genuine interest in me!"

Zen keels over in forced laughter for the benefit of any eavesdroppers.

"HAHAHAHAHAHA. You better watch those jokes, Mel. Don't think the tabloids won't run with the 'best friends with benefits' story! HAHAHAHAHA." Then, as he's bent over in these exaggerated hysterics, he whispers, "You're talking too much tonight. What's gotten into you?"

I give him a cutting look. "What's gotten into me? Nothing." I look down at my belly. "Nothing has gotten into me at all."

"You think it's been easy for me to see you with him?"

I *know* he doesn't like seeing me with Jondoe any more than I like seeing him get hit on by one humpy girl after another. And yet I have trouble feeling much sympathy for him for one really, *rilly* good reason.

"You need stop talking immediately," Zen says in a serious voice. "Because it's not just about you. Think about your sister."

"My sister. Who could deliver at any moment in Goodside." I pause dramatically. *"Where she has chosen to stay put."*

"There's still time for her to change her mind."

Isn't that exactly what I tried to tell Jondoe earlier this evening?

"I'm telling you, Melody," he says, his eyes nervously scanning the room to make sure no one is listening, "you have built yourself a powerful platform, and when you finally get to speak, millions—no, billions—of girls will listen and rise up and demand . . ."

And before Zen can go full manifesto, Lib is all up in our facespace again.

"WHY ARE YOU HERE BUT TO TORTURE ME?"

Again, someone else says what I cannot.

"I can't find Jondoe anywhere," Lib whispers before going back to a full shout. "THIS IS TOTALLY UNPROFESSIONAL."

"This may not even be a bad thing after all," Zen offers. "The MiNet will go wild with speculation. . . ."

Lib finishes the thought for him. "WONDERING WHY JONDOE IS A NO-SHOW!" Then he grudgingly gives Zen a look of approval.

"Aren't either of you at all curious as to where he might be?" I ask.

I'm getting legitimately worried now. Jondoe's synapses weren't firing at maximum capacity tonight.

"Don't worry, gorgeous." Lib pats my head. "He can't stay off-grid forever. And when we find him, there will be a whole new surge in optics!" He tips back his head and cackles. "You know, it's such genius publicity it's almost like I planned it! And you know what? I'll take credit for it anyway!"

I'd be offended if his superficial fame-gaming wasn't so predictable. In a way, I've got to admire his transparency.

At least Lib is exactly who he appears to be. Right now I can't say that about anyone else in my inner circle.

"You think you can do this by yourself?" Lib asks.

I nod. I can do this in my sleep.

Without a second's hesitation, Lib runs out of the room to let the tech crew know that this will be a solo performance after all. The DJ downstairs is now playing The Hotties' dance version of the Babiez R U theme song, pop music being an obvious revenue stream with our names and all. If I weren't so wanked out right now, I might find it amusing to see Ram leading hundreds of partiers playing air guitar and singing out loud:

We're the most important girls on the planet! The most powerful girls on the planet! The prettiest most popular most princessy most everything girls on the planet!

And for the past eight and a half months, it's all been true.

But not for much longer.

I'm taking a fortifying swig of soda when the door opens again. I'm dreading the reappearance of Ventura and her peaking ovaries when in walks a couple that's like, old. They've got to be in their thirties at least. *So* not my target demo. But as soon as they enter the room, they crane their necks looking for someone and I automatically know that person is me. Sure enough, the woman finds me on the opposite side of the room and rushes over with her partner.

I sigh and elbow Zen in the ribs. It's another couple that wants to cash in on The Hotties' fame and fortune.

"Melody Mayflower!" the woman gushes. "We've waited for this moment for such a long time!"

I stop them before they can even start their spiel.

"Take the YDNA test," I tell them.

They look at each other, baffled.

"What?" they ask at the same time.

"You think I'm your long-lost daughter, right?" I say, not waiting for them to reply. "You need to take the YDNA test to prove it. They should have told you that before they let you in here."

I know I sound harsh. But you would be jaded too if you had been confronted by hundreds of counterfeiting couples claiming to be your long-lost birthparents.

Now that I've actually gotten a close look at the woman, I see she's actually quite attractive in the all-natural surgical aesthetic that's the opposite of what's trending for obsolescents these days. I mean, like, every twentysomething Team Hottie intern has erased all outward traces of her genetic identity with forehead extensions, skin dyes, and nasal implants, but this woman's face is refreshingly *human*. There's something else about the stranger's appearance that makes me linger longer over her features—clear blue eyes, high cheekbones, pert nose, full lips—and it takes me a few seconds to figure out what it is: She looks a lot like me. A *lot*. Only like, as I said, waaaay older. I'm so relieved Harmony isn't here right now because there would be nothing stopping her from jumping into this woman's lap and calling her "Mama." I almost wouldn't blame her because as far as fakers go, this one is undoubtedly the best I've seen so far. Her partner—who is just average-looking, and losing his hair—is surely the brains of this operation.

They look at each other again and laugh nervously.

"You don't know who we are?" the woman asks.

"No idea," I say.

"We're the Jaydens!" the husband says.

"And these," says the wife, framing my belly with her hands, "are our daughters!"

The MOM alarm goes crazy.

Bleeeeeeeep! Bleeeeeeep! Bleeeeeep!

Zen instinctively puts his arms around my shoulders to bolster me from the blow that's just been leveled right at me. Because if I really *were* carrying their daughters, I'd probably break water right now.

But I'm not.

Which leaves me no choice but to confront the two biggest victims of The Hotties' scam, who I never considered victims until they were grinning right in front of me.

harmony
melody

THE BARN IN THE BACKYARD IS ASTIR WITH WARNINGS.

Mooing, clucking, whinnying, bleating.

Knock knock knock knock.

There it is. The arrival at the front door that I've been waiting for.

As I make my way down the stairs, I think about how it used to be. Before I went Wayward, I was never without the company of my prayerclique, a chaperone, or a spying housebrother . . . or ten! But now I don't get visitors. Today's nesting party was an exception—and look how well that turned out. I may be sought-after on the other side of the gates, but Goodside is the only place on the planet I'm guaranteed to be left in peace. The fame that attracts millions of MiNet followers is the same fame that keeps the whole settlement—even my own ma—at a distance. Oh, I still get the invitations to quilting bees and canning parties. But the chairs next to me go empty until filled by latecomers who always make an effort to arrive earlier next time. I don't hold any ill will for them in my heart. If I were like the other girls, I'd be frightened of me too.

I reach the front entrance and take a deep breath before opening the door to four men wearing black hats, black suits, black boots. They are the most powerful Elders on the Church Council and their faces are interchangeably grim beneath their graying beards.

"Where is the man of the house?" asks the first Councilman I privately call Elder Blather because his sermons are always too long on time and too short on substance. I knew better than to share this observation with my housesisters, though Ram thought it was both funny and true.

"He's not here," I say. "He's away on special missionary business in Goodside."

The Elders are visibly uncomfortable now. It's considered improper for any man to have a conversation with another man's wife in his absence. It's not against the Orders exactly, but it's definitely frowned upon because such fraternizing can court temptation. And I'm not just any wife, mind you, but easily the most infamous young woman who has ever dwelled in this settlement or any other. No girl has ever come back after going Wayward for as long as I did. No girl has ever encouraged as many conversions or donations to the Church either. In short, the

Elders don't know what to make of my mixed blessings. For such black-and-white thinkers, I am too much gray.

"You received yet another call from an unapproved Othersider earlier this evening, did you not?"

The Elders show up on my doorstep whenever Jondoe tries to reach me. So this question isn't unexpected.

"I did," I say. "But I didn't answer it."

I wanted to. Oh, how I wanted to. But I didn't.

"That is of no matter. Are you courting devilry, Harmony?"

I expected this too. I pinch my mouth closed, shake my head no. Though I'm not sure whether I'm being honest or not.

"Do you have God, Harmony?"

I nod yes. This is true.

"Your prayerclique fears for your soul."

I know this. Every day I've put in the effort to circle up with my prayerclique and call for those things that only bring glory to God. But oh my grace it's difficult to keep my heart and mind open when I am repeatedly made the "anonymous" target of those prayers. I was a little more than a month into my return when I made what I thought was an innocent comment about the floor-length, full-sleeved dresses we're required to wear in accordance with the Orders.

"Wouldn't it be a relief if we could wear sleeveless dresses in the summertime?"

I was only in my first trimester then, and yet my skin

felt hot and tight, like a sausage on a stick over the fire. (More than once that sweltering summer, I'd wonder if there was a connection between the heat I felt in my body and the hellfire in my soul.)

The very next morning, Emily was quick to make an offer to open the prayershare.

"Please pray for my friend who wants to wear provocative clothing instead of modest attire." Then she made a point of glancing knowingly around the circle, pausing long enough at me for everyone to notice. She pursed her lips before adding, "Girls who are devoted to God make themselves attractive not by what they wear, but by the good things they *do*."

I should have put out of my mind right then that I could ever raise more serious questions about Church doctrine. But I kept hoping. I thought maybe, just maybe, I could find someone else here who sought a different relationship with God. I've only recently begun to accept that I'm the sole doubter among us.

And by cutting off my braid, I've confirmed it.

As if he's read my thoughts, a Councilman taps Elder Blather on the shoulder and whispers something in his ear. Elder Blather startles, takes hold of me by the shoulders, and spins me half around so he can see the back of my head.

"You cut your hair," he says, stating the obvious.

I touch the nape of my neck where my braid once was.

"I have," I say.

This results in more murmuring.

"You do understand that this too is in direct defiance of the Orders?"

I nod, oddly unafraid. "I am."

"The Orders exist for you to best serve Him. And yet you insist on repeatedly defying them." Elder Blather bows his head, which is a sign that I should too. "*Let every soul be subject to the governing authorities. For there is no authority except from God, and the authorities that exist are appointed by God.*"

I've heard Romans 13:1 a lot. As a governing authority, this is a very convenient verse for Elder Blather to use on me.

"You'll follow through on your obligations to the ministry tonight, wearing a veil to disguise your disobedience. Tomorrow the MiVu will be permanently removed from your home as you have shown time and again that you are incapable of walking the right path."

"But I—"

He holds up a bony finger to silence me.

"Furthermore, you have left us no choice but to take a vote."

He doesn't finish the sentence. And he can't even bring himself to look me in the face as he lets the unspoken sink in.

They're going to take a vote on my Shunning.

"It is the way of the Lord," he says before departing.

No! I want to protest. *It's the way of the Church.* And

that isn't the same thing at all. But why am I the only one who sees it that way? I was a fool to think that I could ever fulfill my feminine promise as if I had never left. I'm not like Ma, or my housesisters, or my prayerclique, and I never have been. And it's not because I'm adopted, because the Church has taken in dozens of the sickest or otherwise difficult-to-place babies over the decades. Katie, for example, had the cord wrapped around her neck and didn't get enough oxygen when she was born and will always be a bit slower than the rest of us. And yet she, like all the other rescued babies, has seamlessly blended with the rest of the settlement. All but me.

If the Church community is like my white-on-white wedding quilt, I'm the lone red square stitched with raggedy twine.

I know the threat of Shunning is supposed to fill me with dread, spur me to repentance and obedience, but it actually has the opposite effect. I feel strangely . . . free. Having a household all to myself was really just a kinder alternative to Shunning all along. What's the difference? The red dress? I don't have to attend prayercliques and quilting bees? Good riddance to all of it!

Oh my grace! Another rebellion of fists and feet.

How could I have forgotten? It's not about me.

"What about the twins?" I shout out to the Elders, who are already halfway down the drive. "What will happen to them?"

Elder Blather turns slowly around, his face ghoulish in the lantern light.

"Our vote," he says coldly, "will determine whether the twins are any concern of yours."

melody

harmony

I'M MOCKED UP.

Yes, it's true. The girl who hated trying on Babiez R U FunBumps has been successfully faking one of the most high-profile preggings in history.

There are only four of us in on the scam: Harmony, Jondoe, Zen, and me. Lib is in on half the truth: He knows Harmony bumped with Jondoe but is happy to uphold the image of the brand by letting everyone else think her deliveries are Ram's. As for Ram, he says he'll raise the babies with Harmony in Goodside because that's what she's asked him to do. As for what he really believes, I don't know. And Harmony has made it clear that she doesn't want me to ask.

The rest of the world thinks we're fulfilling our

obligations as our parents always expected. None of this would have been possible without Jondoe's full cooperation, which he gave for one reason: Harmony.

"She'll change her mind," I had told him eight and a half months ago, when Harmony shocked us all by returning to Goodside with Ram. "She'll come back. And when she does, The Hotties will have earned her enough money to start a whole new life. She'll be free to be whoever she wants to be. . . ."

"I can give her the money she needs to be independent right now!"

"How can she earn her independence if you're the one buying it for her?"

He had almost protested, but thought better of it.

"Won't the Jaydens be pissed when they find out we scammed them? Won't the whole world?"

"Do you care about Harmony or your career?"

He winced. "I wasn't thinking about my career," he said. "I was actually thinking about *you*."

That was when I kind of got why Harmony had fallen for Jondoe. It was the first time I saw him not as a product, but as a real person capable of caring about people other than himself.

"Don't worry about me. Zen and I are working on a plan, *a mission*, really," I had said cryptically. "The world will get over it just fine. Including the Jaydens."

That was so much easier to believe when the Jaydens were anonymous cradlegrabbers. They met me, like, thirty seconds ago and they're already proudly show-ing off pictures of the nursery. They're so off-the-spring excited just to be in close proximity of my belly that it's obvious to me now that they are not going to "get over it" so easily.

"May I . . . ?" asks the Mrs. as she tentatively reaches out to me.

Or rather, to the Billion Dollar Belly.

According to Jondoe, it's a top-secret prototype for a product called Artificial Living Tissue Engineered for Reproducing Reproduction. Eight and a half months ago I applied the transparent film to my midsection and for the past thirty-five weeks it has developed exactly as a real pregnancy would. It's basically the next-generation syn-thetic skinfeel that's used all the time in cosmetic surgery, only the ALTERR cells are encoded with microholo-graphic imaging systems that simulate pregnancy. That's a fancy way of saying it's the most authentic FunBump ever. ALTERR isn't approved for consumer use, so the B$B could swell to ten times its size, swallow me whole, and launch a parasitic attack on New Jersey.

Which doesn't sound too bad right about now.

"I can feel them moving around!" the Mrs. says rhap-sodically.

Of course she can. I've gotten away with avoiding internal exams (to "protect my reproductive privacy") because ALTERR can fool an ultrasound. To my medical team, my twins are every bit as real as Harmony's. I've scammed the whole world.

"Our daughters!"

I'm fooling the Jaydens right now.

I feel like I'm about to puke.

"Are you okay?" the Mr. asks. "You look a little green."

"Have you had morning sickness this whole time?" the Mrs. asks. "Oh, that must be awful!"

Her sympathy makes me feel even sicker.

Zen steps between me and the Jaydens, unexpectedly grabs my hands, and starts pinching the webbing between my thumb and index fingers.

"Let's stimulate those pulse points!" he says in a strained voice. "That'll make the nausea go away!" With his back to the Jaydens, he sends me a loud and clear message with his eyes: Don't do it.

Zen knows me better than anyone. And he knows how close I am to just giving it all up right now. But how can I just sit back and let these people make more plans for these babies *that are never going to come*? Has Zen lost his humanity along with his mind? I don't get another moment to contemplate this question because Lib is zooming across the room and going psycho on the Jaydens.

"What in the name of Darwin are you two doing here?" he seethes through a gritted-teeth smile. "I explicitly told you not to come here under any circumstances."

55

"But . . ." says the Mrs.

"*But nothing*," he whisper-shouts. "This is dangerous. Do you understand? DANGEROUS."

It's true that Surrogettes and Parental Units are discouraged from meeting each other, but the legislation that would make such interactions illegal hasn't passed yet. So I don't know what's gotten into Lib. I mean, it's beyond over the top, even for him.

When the Mrs. withers under Lib's glare, the Mr. steps up.

"Hey, she's been through a lot. Take it easy on her . . ."

"ARE YOU SUGGESTING I DON'T KNOW WHAT SHE'S BEEN THROUGH?"

"Hey Lib, it's cool," Zen says, trying to keep the peace.

"It is ABSOLUTELY and UNDER NO CIRCUMSTANCES cool. And why do you get to have an opinion anyway?" He returns to the Jaydens. "Please leave now before you jeopardize everything I've worked for."

The Mrs. is crying and the Mr. looks like he's on the verge of joining her. I have no idea why Lib is overreacting like this.

"I'm sorry," the Mr. is saying. "We'll leave. Of course we'll leave. We'd never do anything to ruin . . ."

"Then do exactly as I tell you," Lib all but whispers, as if he's got no voice left.

And before I can even apologize for Lib getting all ragey, he leads them to the door. But what makes this weird situation even weirder is how he puts his arms around them as he does it. It's a surprisingly tender gesture, considering the circumstances.

I have just enough time to warn everyone in my radius.

"I'm gonna throw up."

Then I lean over and heave into the nearest recycling bin.

harmony
melody

ELDER BLATHER'S MENACING PROCLAMATION IS FAR MORE life-changing than anything he's ever said from the pulpit.

It's not what I wanted to hear. But it's exactly what I *needed* to hear.

I imagine Katie, Emily, and Laura have already eagerly agreed to stay up all night to sew me a tented red maternity dress that will be ready for me to wear in the morning. My own ma might even help them with the measurements. A true believer must accept her punishment, with child or not.

When I was about thirteen I once asked Ma about Shunning, and why the men on the Council were allowed to pass Judgment when the Bible says that only God has the power to do so. That was before I realized that I couldn't turn to Ma when I was in spiritual crisis because she has unchanging faith in the Church. Ma told me to stop asking such questions because I would be deemed unmarriageable. She was right. Not long after I asked that question—and others like it—the Council voted against my first engagement to a stranger named Shep and arranged for him to marry my more compliant housesister.

The Church Council had to pass Shep's homestead on the way to mine, lanterns lighting the way, alerting them and the entire settlement to my latest transgressions. How grateful Shep must be now that I'm Ram's problem, not his. In the years after that failed engagement and before my marriage to Ram, I used to hide in the fields with my bird-watching binoculars and catch glimpses of happy families in their windows as they lived their prayerful and harmonious lives. I would search for signs of discord on their faces, in their actions, hoping to find an ally. But I never did.

And I never will.

I'm overcome by the urge to do something far more radical than cutting my hair, something I've resisted doing since the last days of spring and all through the long summer and fall. It's winter now, the days are shorter than ever. I'm acutely aware, way down deep in my aching bones, that my time is running out. The Elders have confirmed that I have more to lose by doing nothing at all.

I pray for the strength I need to make the call.

It's an old-model MiVu, so I have to type Melody's

code into the keypad. It's like I've always known that it would be used for this very purpose, as if that were the only reason I ever had it at all.

I need to leave.

I need help.

I need my sister.

melody
harmony

MY STOMACH IS STILL CHURNING, AND I'M DIZZY WITH REGRET.

"Don't do this to yourself," Zen warns, offering me a glass of water.

"I can feel bad about this." My hand is shaking, and water splashes over the lip.

"No, you can't," he says.

"You know what? I'm tired of you telling me what I can and cannot do. My parents were never as bad as you are right now."

This really isn't true. The first sixteen years of my life were spent following a very specific list of things I could and could not do, all of which were prescribed by a panel of experts outsourced by my parents in the attempt to make me into the top Surrogette they believe I am today. This is the foundation on which my parents' new business—if not their whole existence—lies. Which is why the truth will rock them harder than anyone.

Well, except the Jaydens. Ohhh, the Jaydens . . .

"I'll tell you why you don't have to feel sorry for the Jaydens," Zen whispers. "Because everyone else on the MiNet *will* feel sorry for the Jaydens. And they'll line themselves up another top Surrogette so fast, they won't even have time to get mad at you."

I wish I still believed what Zen was saying. Now that I've met them—and they've met me—it's just not that simple anymore. They're real people who have fallen madly in love with these fake twins.

Throughout this whole scam, I've tried not to think about how the Jaydens would react when they found out the truth. It was easy not to care, really, when Lib had made them seem like such status-obsessed famegamers. This was a couple that was so fixated on perfection that they waited eighteen months—made *me* wait eighteen months!—while they waited for their application to be finally accepted by Jondoe. Only the hottest RePro on the MiNet was good enough for their "couture conception," which is ironic because they were nowhere near good enough for him. Jondoe took them on as charitable pro-boner work just to give his image a boost and he ended up getting so much more than he bargained for.

Didn't we all?

The thing is, the Jaydens I had imagined were very

different from the people who set up a nursery in their brand-new home in a neighborhood selected for its excellent school system and acres of greenspace.

I *liked* these people. If I had to choose between my own parents and them, I'd totally have to give them the thumbs-up.

More horrifying than that?

I know they will make awesome parents.

Would make awesome parents.

If . . .

And a second round of nausea has me dry-heaving headfirst into the recyclables.

"WHAT'S going ON with you tonight?" Lib asks as I try to breathe normally.

"I could ask the same of you, Lib," I somehow manage to say. "You went off on the Jaydens for no good reason. Zen was right. They seemed really cool and . . ."

Lib exhales so sharply that I'm surprised his nose doesn't blast off his face.

"Listen, doll," he says in a soft voice that is far more effective than his screech. "Just because *you* don't know the reason doesn't mean there isn't one. There is no one more invested in your contract with the Jaydens than I am. NO ONE." He takes my hands in his and looks me deep in the eyes. "You have to trust me. You do trust me, don't you? Because I've put my trust in you in a PROFOUND way, Miss Melody Mayflower. And I hope you would do the same with me."

He breaks away for a moment, blinking wildly. At first I think he's scanning the MiNet, but then I realize that he's trying to stop himself from crying. I haven't seen him this emotional since the day he told me I was bumping with Jondoe.

The thing is, I don't trust Lib to look out for my best interests. He's proven to care about one thing only, and that's the bottom line. Last spring, when he discovered that Jondoe and Harmony had run off with each other, his first instinct was to write me off as a bad investment and to woo my sister into taking my place. When Zen, Jondoe, and I had our first strategic discussions about The Hotties, we debated for a long time as to what we should do about Lib. Ultimately, we decided it would be safer to make him a *part* of the lie without letting him in on it. We told him that Jondoe had bumped *both* of us, but Harmony was in denial and insisted that Ram was the real father and that they would stay in Goodside and raise the babies as their own. We pointed out that this miraculous, once-in-many-lifetimes identical twin synchro-bump had serious branding potential, if only someone had the business smarts to pull it all together for us. We all assumed that by the time Lib found out I was faking it, his earnings from The Hotties would be so beyond what he would've made in the original deal with the Jaydens that he'd swoon in admiration of our capitalistic vision and express eternal gratitude for giving him such a generous percentage of the profits.

He sniffs, then continues.

"All I'm saying is, you can trust me. Your health and well being, and those precious deliveries, are my top priority. I would never do anything to put you—or them—in jeopardy."

Gah. I never thought I'd feel even the littlest bit bad about scamming Lib. But all this talk of trust? And his sense of responsibility for not just me, but my *deliveries*? He's never spoken like this before. He's never cared about what happened to a delivery from the moment it took its first breath. Why is he starting now? He doesn't sound anything like the Lib I've known since I was thirteen.

"Well, I'll go make a statement."

And then Lib takes off, preparing to spin our latest lie. Everything is back to normal, but nothing feels right.

Zen has just returned to the couch with a cold compress in his hand.

"I know you're under a lot of stress right now," Zen's saying, gently resting the damp napkin on my forehead. "I promise nothing bad will happen to you."

"You can't guarantee that!"

"You have to look at the bigger picture. . . ."

I shush him, and not only because I'm still feeling pukey and for seriously not in the mood to listen to him go manifesto about how I'm destined to be a feminist icon for the ages or whatever, but also because I've got an incoming message.

"It's Harmony!" I say, but quietly. Lib cleared the room

at my request, but gossipmongers abound.

"Mellllloooooodeeee," Harmony wails, and then the rest of her sentence is swallowed by strange choking sounds.

"What's wrong?"

And when she responds with even more horrifying animal howling than before, I know that this must have to do with Jondoe. Harmony has made it beyond clear that she wants no contact with Jondoe in facespace or on the MiNet or anywhere else.

"I told Jondoe not to contact you," I say.

"THIS ISN'T ABOUT JONDOE." The audio in my earbuds gets all fuzzy. "It's the twins . . ." she moans. "The twins . . ."

"Did your water break?"

My skin prickles at the thought of it: This could all be over very soon.

"NOOOOO."

"Then what's wrong?"

"They're going to take the twins!"

"Who?"

"The Church!" she spits out. "You have to come get me!"

I don't know what's going on, but if Harmony wants me to spring her from Goodside I don't need the details.

"I'm leaving right now!"

And then our connection goes dead.

When I try to spring into action, Zen throws an arm across my chest to keep me on the couch.

"What's happening? Where are you going?"

"Harmony needs my help."

Zen searches my face. "Are you hiding something from me? Did her water break? Because if it did, we need to set the Mission in motion. . . ."

"Enough about the Mission, already!" I yell, lifting his arm off me. "I'm so sick of hearing about the stupid mission."

"It's not stupid! Shifting paradigms is not stupid!"

And that's when I do the most insulting thing possible: I laugh right in his face.

"Oh, that's really mature, Melody."

"I'm the one acting immature? I'm not the one throwing a tantrum right now—"

"You know what? I'm not under contract! I'm a free agent! I don't have to put up with this!"

"Then *don't*!"

And in the middle of this drama enters the last person on the planet I'd want to see us fighting like this.

"Am I interrupting something?" Ventura purrs.

I must look like I'm about to puke again because Lib rushes back into the room and right over to me with a wastepaper basket.

"What can I do to make it all better, gorgeous?" he asks me, holding back my hair. "Just say the word. I'm a DOER. I make things happen."

Can he make Ventura Vida disappear? Doubtful.

"Hey ya'll," Ram drawls, blissfully unaware of the chaos

he's moseying into. "Was that a barn raiser or *what*?"

He must have been in the direct blast zone of a glitter bomb, because he is covered head to toe in pink sparkles. His arrival is just about the best thing that's happened to me all night.

"Ram!" I jump up and hug him, a decision I immediately regret when I see the sweaty glitter slick left in the wake of our embrace.

"We have to go to Goodside immediately. Harmony needs us," I say.

Regret crushes Ram's face. "I knew I shouldn't have left her alone tonight." He takes off his hat and smacks himself in the head with it.

"DID HER WATER BREAK?" Lib asks.

"No!" I say. "She just needs my company."

"Well, I'm coming with you!" Lib insists.

"You won't make it past the gate," Ram warns.

"That's right," I say. "They love their God and they love their guns. They will shoot you first and pray for forgiveness later."

"It's true," Ram says, wiping his wet brow with the back of hand, cutting a clean streak through the glitter. "Now, come on, let's go! We're wasting time!"

I'll tell you who *isn't* wasting any time: Ventura Vida. She must have mega-dosed on Tocin or some other love drug in the bathroom because she's given up on subtleties and is pressing herself against Zen in a predatory way, like she's ravenously hungry and Zen is dinner. His eyes are closed, but hers are wide open . . . and glaring right at me.

I should be out the door already but my legs won't move. I stare right back at her. Not because I want to but because I can't look away. I need to watch Ventura steal Zen. I've lied to so many people about so many things, it only seems fitting that something—someone—so pure should be taken away from me.

I'm getting exactly what I deserve.

I can't say how long we're locked in this staredown. Long enough to think about me and Zen riding bikes to school together, me and Zen quizzing each other for the Science Olympiad, me and Zen laughing over secrets in our plastic tree house. Long enough to recall how his lips felt on mine, the first and only time we kissed. To remember the sizzle of electricity when our hands touched. . . .

Bleeeeeeeep! Bleeeeeeeep! Bleeeeeeeep!

He's my best friend but I don't even bother saying good-bye.

Zen's already gone.

SECOND

"Whoever can be trusted with very little can also be trusted with much, and whoever is dishonest with very little will also be dishonest with much."

—Luke 16:10

melody
harmony

ONE ADVANTAGE TO MY FAME IS ACCESS TO THE FASTEST first-class transportation. This autopiloted air taxi to Goodside will only take fifteen minutes, which is just enough time for me to get in costume and in character.

"It's safe to look now!" I command Ram, who insisted on covering his eyes while I changed. "What do you think?"

There isn't a lot of room in the cabin, but I do a slow, clumsy spin to model the Conception Couture maternity gown Lib borrowed from a vendor at the party. We figure it will be easier to sneak me into Goodside if I'm dressed as Harmony.

Ram inspects me carefully. "You don't have freckles on your nose like she does," he says. "But I doubt anyone else will notice."

Jondoe would notice, I think. I feel bad that he's not here with us right now, but that's his own fault for going off the grid. Besides, Jondoe and Ram have gone out of their way to avoid each other for the past eight and a half months. Now certainly isn't the time for Harmony's husband and babydaddy to bond.

"How are we going to get her out of there?"

"It's Sunday night. Zeke Yoder will be at the main gate," he says. "He'll let us in and out if we're right quick about it."

I'm relying entirely on Ram here. I have to trust him, but he's not the sharpest pitchfork in the barn.

"How do you know?"

Ram reveals the tiniest hint of a smile. "I just know is all."

My own sketchiness has made me more attuned to others' secret-keeping. There's definitely something Ram isn't telling me right now.

"It sounds like you've got experience with sneaking around," I say in a leading way that I hope will encourage him to keep talking.

"I reckon I do." He blushes. Then, to take the heat off himself, he asks, "So what's going on with you and Zen anyway? That other girl was getting mighty familiar."

Gaaah. My stomach swoops and drops, and it's not because the air taxi has just flown through a turbulent air stream.

"I don't know anymore," I say honestly.

Zen was right when he said he isn't contractually obligated to do anything with anyone. He's a free agent. He doesn't have to wait around for me. He can sperminate anyone he wants to.

Or no one at all.

Zen *is* still in possession of one black-market condom, after all. He wouldn't use it with Ventura, would he? WOULD HE? Because as eager as she is to bump, Zen is equally committed to the Mission.

The *stupid* mission.

"We're almost there!" Ram calls out as the air taxi slows down its descent. "Just let me do all the talking."

Ram has changed dramatically since I've known him. Eight and a half months ago, Zen and I had to dose Ram with Tocin just to get more than monosyllabic responses out of him. Now he's masterminding escape plans. These public appearances have really helped him come out of his shell.

The air taxi decelerates considerably before hovering over the green space in front of the main gates to Goodside. Ram glances out the window.

"Oh dear Lord!" he yelps, unbuckling himself from the seat.

And before I can even ask what's wrong, he slams open the Emergency Exit door. The air taxi is still hovering a good ten feet in the air, but that doesn't stop Ram from jumping out and landing with a roll onto the grass.

"Ram!" I scream. "Are you crazy?"

I try to get a look at what's going on outside. Ram quickly picks himself up and runs toward two other men at the entrance to the settlement. It's too dark and distant to see what's going on and I have to impatiently wait a few seconds for the taxi to finally touch down. I dart out the door as soon as it's landed, and try to move as fast as I can toward the scene of the commotion, which isn't easy to do in this ankle-length gown. I don't know how Harmony has put up with this dress code for so long.

"Put the gun down, Zeke!" Ram is shouting.

"I'VE GOT A TRESSPASSER!" squawks a tall, skinny guard pointing the gun at a third bearded man in black with his hands up in surrender. What is this? A bit of Church-on-Church infighting? A ruckus over a stolen goat or whatever Goodsiders feud over?

"Don't shoot! I know him! He's with me!" Ram shouts, putting himself in front of the human target.

This seems to agitate Zeke even more. "What do you mean *with you*?"

The barrel of the gun is shaking. If Zeke aims for the heart, the bullet just might miss Ram altogether.

"Now is not the time for this, Zeke," Ram says in an assertive tone I've never heard before.

"When *is* the time for it?"

"Not when you're carrying a loaded shotgun!"

"Who is he, anyway? Is he from another settlement?"

There's something odd going on between these two, and it has absolutely nothing to do with me or the captured man in question. The trespasser must also be picking up on the strange tension, because he lifts his head and smiles bemusedly at me.

And that's when I see him for who he really is.

It's Jondoe in disguise.

That crazy, lovestruck sonuvahump is here to free Harmony too.

harmony
melody

I'M SCURRYING AROUND THE HOUSE, TRYING TO DECIDE WHAT I should pack (cloth diapers, knitted booties, cotton jumpers?) and what I should leave behind (cloth diapers, knitted booties, cotton jumpers?) when I'm stopped in my tracks by the lowing and braying of the animals in the barn.

Someone's coming. Again.

I peek out the front hall window and see three lantern lights approaching my driveway. Oh my grace. The Elders! They must know that I've called my sister! Will they force me to stay here until the twins are born? It would have been better for everyone if I had never come back here. But it's too late now. For a brief moment I consider making a run for it. But at eight and a half months pregnant, I'm not going to get very far very fast.

There's nowhere for me to hide, nothing more for me to do but slump into a kitchen chair and surrender.

I'm helpless. Hopeless.

The lights reach the front landing. There's no knock, just rattling of the doorknob.

"Open up!" I'd recognize that squawk anywhere: It's Zeke Yoder. Unarmed, he's about as intimidating as a baby chick. With a shotgun, however, he's the most dangerous man in the settlement.

"It's me, Harmony!"

Oh my grace. It's Melody! She came just like she promised! She must have been stopped by Zeke at the front gate. I wonder why he didn't turn her in to the Elders straightaway.

And then the bearer of the third light speaks.

"And me."

Are my ears playing tricks on me?

For the first time since I returned to Goodside, I don't feel weighted down by hopelessness. I turn the lock and allow myself to acknowledge this feeling—a wish, really—as to whose voice I heard, and who it might be on the other side.

Please, please, please, I silently ask a God who should have stopped listening to me long ago.

I open the door to find my sister looking just like me in a green maternity gown.

"Harmony," she gasps. "Your hair!"

Well, *almost* like me.

Next to her stands Zeke, who is dwarfed by a second bearded man dressed in a black hat and black suit. His identity is unmistakable, if inexplicable.

Jondoe.

And yet, in that Goodside suit, with an abundant fake beard, he doesn't look all that different from Ram or any other young man in the settlement. It's easy to convince myself, if only for a moment or two, that he is the Church member in good standing that I married eight and a half months ago, not Ram.

Until he smiles at me with those startlingly white teeth.

Jondoe's teeth are brighter and straighter than anyone's in Goodside have ever been, or ever will be. He illuminates the porch better than any lamplight, and it feels like my every prayer has been answered. And though I know I shouldn't under these serious circumstances, I can't help but smile back.

Zeke clears his throat. "These Othersiders say they need to call on you, Sister."

My tongue is trapped in my throat.

I haven't said a word to Jondoe since the morning after our one night together, when I slipped out the window and ran away. I remember how angry I was that morning, how humiliated and betrayed I felt after giving Jondoe the part of myself that I was supposed to save for my husband.

"She's my sister," I say. "And I know him."

And it's only after the words have left my lips and reached Jondoe's ears that the alternative meaning of those words come to mind.

Oh yes, I know him. I have known him.

I blush. And unless I'm imagining things, I see red creeping across Jondoe's cheeks too, just above his counterfeit beard.

"Ram said they want you to minister to them."

"He did?" Then I redirect the question to Jondoe and Melody. "You *what*?"

"We came to convert," Melody says, clasping her hands together at her chest.

"Yes," Jondoe adds. "We want to join the Church."

The sound of his voice makes me woozy. I close my eyes in a long, exhausted blink.

"Reckon I'll leave you to it," I hear Zeke say. "I gotta get back to my post."

I listen to Zeke's footsteps fade away. When I slowly open my eyes again, Jondoe is all I can see.

"Harmony."

I try to focus on his face.

"Jondoe."

Oh, what a joy to say his name again, not hidden behind a pronoun. All these months I've been unable to resist talking about Jondoe in the only way I knew how: by praying for his anonymous soul in prayerclique.

Please pray for a man who put his material riches before Heaven's rewards.

Please pray for a man who shared his body outside the marriage bed.

Please pray for a man who lied to the girl who loved him.

Every time I clasped hands and looked Heavenward in secret prayer, my heart sprang up and sang inside me:

I'm praying for you, Jondoe! Can you hear me?

He heard me. And now he's here.

His face is the last thing I see before all the lights go out.

melody

harmony

JONDOE CATCHES HARMONY BEFORE SHE DROPS TO THE FLOOR.

"What's wrong with her?"

"She's obviously in shock!" I say, helping Jondoe pull Harmony's limp body into a sitting position. "I told you it would be too much for her! You should've waited with Ram in the air taxi!"

"Oh, sure!" he says, as he frantically fans Harmony's face. "So he could borrow Zeke's shogun and blast my balls off!"

"He just saved your life, remember?"

Ram told Zeke that Jondoe and I had paid big money to be ministered by Harmony in person. He also convinced him not to turn us in to the Elders until after we'd accepted the Lord.

"They'll know you were responsible for the highest-profile conversions in the Church history!" Ram had claimed.

From the skeptical look on his face, it seemed less likely that Zeke obliged because he believed what Ram was saying, but more because Ram is the one who had asked him to believe it. Zeke did insist that it was his duty to escort us to Harmony's household while Ram covered his post. I'm just relieved he was so eager to get back to it. Again, I'm guessing that had more to do with some business with Ram than with us. Zeke made Ram promise that they would "have a talk" when he returned. I can't help but think that Zeke is going to be very disappointed when he gets back to find Ram already gone. The whole incident made no sense to me; then again, very little on this side of the gates did.

"I don't know," Jondoe is saying now as he fans Harmony's face with his hands. "Ram could have spared me just to have the pleasure of punishing me for sleeping with his wife!"

"Ram wouldn't do that," I say. "He's not the vengeful type."

"Blessed are the peacemakers," Harmony mumbles, her eyes fluttering open.

"Harmony!" I exclaim, relieved that she's come to. "We're here to take you out of here. Ram should be here any second with the air taxi. . . ."

The words aren't out of my mouth when I hear the

buzz of the air taxi. Something must be wrong because Ram is standing at the open hatch, gesturing frantically for us to get inside. Jondoe doesn't need to be told what to do. He simply scoops Harmony up into his arms and carries her out the door and across the yard.

"Oh my grace!" Harmony shrieks.

This is serious business, and yet the expressions on both of their faces can only be described as ecstatic, in the truest sense of that word.

"The Elders are on their way out here!" Ram shouts. "We have to go now."

Harmony is pulled inside first, then me, followed by Jondoe. It's only a two-seater, so for a few awkward seconds we're all kind of stumbling all over each other to try to fit inside the tiny cabin. The taxi lifts and dips, lifts and dips, in a struggle to take off.

"Oh no," Jondoe groans. "We must be over the maximum weight limit."

Harmony's eyes fly open in panic. "It's the Elders!" She points out the window at the truck tearing down her driveway. "They're going to force me stay! They're going to take the babies away!" Such vehicles are used only in emergencies, so it's safe to assume that Harmony is right.

The taxi is still wobbling in midair, just a few feet off the ground.

"I'm not going to let that happen to you!" Jondoe says.

"No!" Ram says pushing past Jondoe and toward the door. "*I'm* not going to let that happen to you!"

He reaches behind him and thrusts a small canvas ruck-sack into Harmony's hands.

"This is for you! Use it well!"

And before we can do anything to stop him, Ram jumps out of the air taxi and we zoom upward and away.

harmony
melody

I'M SPEECHLESS.

I can't believe my husband just did that. We've always had a special if not traditional matrimonial bond. All this time I thought I was protecting *him* by pretending.

"Harmony."

I can't bring myself to look at Jondoe. Maybe it's unfair, but I have to ask: If he really cared, wouldn't he have jumped first?

Jondoe crouches down and puts his hand on my knee. I shrink at his touch.

"Please don't." I clutch the unopened canvas bag to my chest like child would hug a rag doll.

"But . . ." he splutters. "I'm just so happy to see you. . . ."

Melody puts an arm around me, as if to shield me from his advances.

"Not now, Jondoe."

"But it's not like that!"

"I know," Melody says. "But I think this reunion is just a little more than my sister can handle right now."

She's right. I close my eyes and take comfort in her company. I try to forget there's anyone else in this cabin but the two of us. My sister and me.

melody
harmony

NO ONE SAYS ANYTHING FOR THE REST OF THE TRIP BACK TO
Princeton. I assume Harmony and Jondoe are lost in
their own thoughts, as I am in mine. *What's happening
to Ram? What will happen with Harmony, Jondoe, and the
twins?* And finally, reluctantly, *What has happened with
Zen and Ventura?*

Once inside my house, I turn to Jondoe.

"Can you give us some time alone?"

Harmony is totally closed off. She drops the canvas
rucksack onto the kitchen countertop, hugs her belly, keeps
her eyes to the floor.

"Sure," he says, trying to paste on a cheerful smile.
"Whatever Harmony needs! I'll be in my room!" He slams
the door behind him harder than necessary.

"His room?" Harmony asks.

I explain that my house has served as Jondoe's unofficial home base ever since she went back to Goodside.

"It was good for keeping up appearances," I say. "He also thought that you'd eventually come around to leaving Goodside and that this would be the first place you'd show up. He wanted to be here when you did."

Harmony nods slowly. "Well, he was right."

"I guess he was."

"I was, wasn't I?" shouts Jondoe from the opposite side of the wall.

Harmony's mouth twitches. I take her by the arm and lead her to my parents' bedroom on the opposite side of the house where we can talk in private.

"Jondoe can't hear us in here."

Harmony takes in the perfectly unrumpled bed, the clutter-free if dusty dressers and beside tables, the foto collage with pictures of me that are no less than two years old.

"Where are your parents?" she asks.

"Oh, they're off building their brand," I say, not really wanting to elaborate.

After I got famous, requests came in from desperate parents all over the country begging Ash and Ty to share their secrets for raising a super-successful Surrogette—like me. Thus, BestEgg was born, a private counseling service "empowering girls to maximize their financial and reproductive potential." My parents travel all over the country developing personalized training programs "from infancy

90

to puberty" that will transform anyone's daughter into a prime candidate for a triple-platinum-level Conception Contract—like mine. In addition to the income they earn as counselors, my parents get a finder's fee for referring the most reproaesthetical girls to Lib. Lib, in turn, posts the top profiles on Hatched.com, his subscription-only site for potential parental units shopping around for their perfect Surrogette.

"You haven't told them the truth?" Harmony asks, sitting down on the edge of the bed that hasn't been slept in for months.

"No," I say. "They're actually avoiding me until after I deliver. They're afraid of Phantom Grandparent Syndrome."

"What?"

It's not surprising that she hasn't heard of this relatively new phenomenon. Even with the suggested regimen of therapeutic and pharmaceutical interventions, many RePros' parents find themselves inexplicably saddened by the giving away of what would have been their grandchildren. The shock of their own conflicted feelings has even inspired Ash and Ty to develop a special seminar, "Giving Up Your Grandchild, Giving Up the Guilt." That Ash and Ty are genuinely afraid of getting all cradlegrabby is baffling to me, because they've never really liked being around kids. Myself included.

I try not to think too much about how they'll react when they find out I've betrayed my brand.

And theirs.

I eagerly change the subject, not that the next topic is any easier than the last.

"What's your plan?"

"My plan?"

Okay. Maybe it was unreasonable for me to think that Harmony had figured this all out. After all, it's only been about a half hour since she decided to leave behind the only life she has ever known, and everything she has been brought up to be and to believe.

"I'm thrilled that you're here, it's what I've always wanted," I say. "I just wish you had made the decision sooner. So we could have, you know, prepared for the twins' arrival. . . ."

Harmony nods once but doesn't say anything.

As calm as I'm trying to appear on the outside, I'm for seriously freaking out on the inside. She is married to one man and carrying the twins of another. And now she's got two new humans on the way with absolutely no plan for what to do with them after they arrive. Harmony seems about as ready to deliver her twins as *I* am, which is totally wanked because my twins are high-tech holograms and hers are, like, real human beings. We're all liars in this, but Harmony's deception runs deeper because she's got two innocent lives to consider.

"What do you think will happen to Ram in Good-side?" I ask.

"I hope they'll just let him go," she says, her forehead

92

furrowed with worry. "He *is* my husband. And I *am* going to have these babies very soon."

I'm almost afraid to ask this question. But if I don't do it now, I never will.

"He knows the twins aren't his, right?"

Harmony shrugs with a nonchalance that is at odds with the subject matter.

"He never asked."

"He never asked?" I'm losing it. "HE NEVER ASKED?"

Harmony snaps into focus and fixes me with a serious look. "He's my husband, Melody," she says sharply. "He shouldn't have to ask."

Could Ram really convince himself he's the father? Does his denial run that deep? I've never asked for the details of what happened on their honeymoon—the one and only night Harmony and Ram slept in the same bed—but I'm pretty sure they were fully clothed the whole time. Only Jondoe could successfully bump under those impossible circumstances, and he apparently didn't need to go to such heroic lengths to do so.

"What about Jondoe?" Harmony asks. "Does he know?"

"Of course he knows! He's always known. Why do you think he tried to contact you so many times? I've spent the last eight months putting up with his brokenhearted moping over what he knows."

He's written sonnets. He's composed love songs. I can't

tolerate Jondoe when he gets all emo over Harmony because if I let him start, he'll never stop.

She rubs her belly. "He's concerned about the twins then."

"He's concerned about *you*," I say. "And I am too. We need to figure this all out, Harmony. As you just said, you could deliver any day now. . . ."

Harmony yawns, grabbing at the weighty fabric of her maternity gown. "Right now I need to get out of this dress and get some rest."

I pull at the fabric of my copycat version of her same dress. "Me too," I say, now yawning also. "I'll bring you a change of clothes and everything you need."

Harmony purses her lips.

"What?" I ask.

"No one person can provide everything I need," she says with a sad smile.

"Then it's a good thing we're all in this together."

Harmony yawns again. "We'll work it out tomorrow."

I don't like the idea of another day going by without a plan. But Harmony does seem too weary to think straight.

"Jondoe. Ram. The twins. Everything." She presses her palms together. "I promise."

I want to believe her more than I actually do.

harmony
melody

I'M MAKING IMPOSSIBLE PROMISES TO MY SISTER WHEN—OH
my grace—I feel it.

I feel God laying a message in my heart. I'm warm all
over, as if a sunbeam has passed over me, though it's as
black as soot outside. This is the last time it will be like
this between Melody and me. Good, bad, a little bit of
both . . . change is coming.

The twins thump my belly from the inside. They must
feel it too.

I take my sister's hands in mine. She looks startled at
first because neither of us are the touchy-feely type. After
countless hours at work in the fields and in the barns, my
hands will always be rougher than hers. It's one of the few
differences in appearance that the press loves to point out

about us. I also have freckles smattered across my nose. And until very recently, the braid I'd been growing since the day we were born.

Melody's face relaxes and a look crosses her face that resembles something like relief.

"Love you," I say, squeezing her smooth, uncalloused fingers.

"Love you too," she says, squeezing back.

This is the first time we've ever said those words to each other. We've felt it but have never said it. Melody has kept her feelings to herself because she's not the emotional type. And I've kept my feelings to myself because I guess there's still part of me that believes my "godfreakiness" could scare her away. It's actually the first time I've ever said those words out loud to anyone, though I've imagined saying them many, many times to someone else . . . and with an entirely different meaning altogether.

I watch Melody as she walks down the hall and pauses at Jondoe's door. She raps a knuckle on the wood twice before entering. She's probably telling him to leave me alone.

How strange it is, how not even a year ago my sister didn't exist to me.

Neither did Jondoe.

Nor the twins.

The Bible says that nothing on earth remains the same, only God is unchanging. And at this point in time, that's one verse I'm still inclined to believe.

melody
harmony

OH, WHAT A SURPRISE. JONDOE IS BEING MELODRAMATIC.

He's lying on the bed on top of the covers, staring at the ceiling. He's still wearing the fake beard and suit, but the Goodside hat rests on his chest, rising and falling with his every breath.

"Do. Not. Bother. Her. Tonight."

He closes his eyes. Says nothing.

"Did you hear me, Jondoe? I mean it! She's fragile right now."

Jondoe sits up suddenly, eyes ablaze. "What about me?"

Gah. He can be so starcissistic sometimes.

"What about you? Not everything is about you."

He shakes his head. "That's not what I mean! Why am *I* not allowed to be fragile in this situation? I have feelings too! I'm a whole person! I'm not just the sum of my private parts!"

This gives me pause. I had never really considered the effects of professional Sperming on Jondoe's psyche. What teenage guy would turn down the opportunity to get paid to get laid? For all his heartbroken histrionics, I admit that Jondoe's reputation has made it very hard for me to totally accept his pure intentions toward my sister.

I pat his shoulder in what I hope is a comforting way.

"All I'm asking is that you give her tonight to rest and recover. If you really believe what you have with her is real, then you've got your whole future together, right?"

He grumbles in a vaguely affirmative way.

I shut his door behind me.

"I helped myself to your closet."

Harmony is watching me from the doorway to my parents' room. She's already changed into black leggings and a T-shirt. She's running her fingers through her raggedly chopped hair. She looks exactly like me, if I had gotten butchered by my stylist.

"And I look like I've helped myself to yours," I say, tugging at the gown with a laugh.

It's pretty surreal to be standing there as our alternate selves, the girls we could have been if my parents had adopted her and hers had adopted me.

"He promised not to bother you tonight," I assure her.

She says thank you, but I swear I catch what looks like a flicker of disappointment crossing her face. I'm too

98

exhausted to take this up now though, and practically crawl to my bathroom.

Tired as I am, I need to take a shower so I can scrub off all my makeup. I take off the gown I—or Harmony—will never wear again. I avert my eyes from the full-length bathroom mirror and run the hot shower so the glass will steam up quickly. I'm still for seriously icked out by the sight of my ginormity. And it's not, like, a lazy lump of excessive poundage. This thing *gets around*. The B$B is designed to move the way real twins would as this point of gestation, as they must be moving inside Harmony right now. She's never once complained about not having seen her feet since August. But I've never gotten used to seeing myself like this, as if an alien race of parasitic gymnasts have colonized on the other side of my belly button.

Unfortunately, I can't avoid looking at myself once I'm in the shower. The B$B looks every bit as convincing when I'm naked. It's really freaky. As I soap up my body, I can't detect where my abdomen ends and the synthetic skinfeel of the bump begins. These nasty stretch marks had better be part of the illusion or I'm going to need a major skinfeel transplant when this thing is over.

If I didn't know any better, I'd actually believe I was pregging.

Could I be pregging?

Gaaaaah.

Jondoe had warned me that the B$B could mess with my mind. He won't give us any details about how he got it or from whom. All he'll say is that he had been approached by a multinational conglomerate to help find the perfect test subject for it.

And that guinea pig is me.

Of course, I had to ask the obvious question: Why would a corporation in the business of *faking* preggs offer a sneak peek to someone rich and famous for *making* preggs? Well, it turns out that getting mocked up is far more common among certain circles of RePros than anyone on the outside would ever imagine. A top-earning Sperm will fake a pregg (or two, or more) in a desperate bid to delay his inevitable obsolescence and retirement from the industry. The faux Surrogette is usually an aspirational famegamer. She gets paid handsomely for signing on for the con, not to mention a major boost to her brand, which she can later trade up for a career as a singer, actress, or brand ambassador. Apparently, it's kind of an open industry secret. I sometimes wonder if Lib has turned a blind eye to the truth all along. Money talks, sure, but it also shuts up when it has to.

There's also a huge market out there for obsolescents who want to experience pregnancy long after the Virus has shut down their reproductive systems. I can vouch that ALTERR is the closest to the real thing. It's so convincing that I sometimes worry that the joke is really on me, that Jondoe is really that skilled and has succeeded where other Sperms before him have only failed: the fabled insemination without penetration. Maybe this bump is legit and

I'm, like, already dilating and about to deliver the world's most anticipated twins *any day now*.

I doubt I'd be any less prepared for the occasion than Harmony is.

Gaaah. This is crazy talk. I just need to finish up here in the shower and go to sleep because I'm beyond exhausted from all of the drama. Harmony and Jondoe. Ram and Zeke. The Jaydens. Lib. Ventura.

Zen.

"Hey, Mel."

ZEN!

harmony
melody

I LIE ON TOP OF THE COVERS, IN THE DARK, EVERY FLESHY inch of me achingly awake and alive. It's impossible to sleep, knowing that Jondoe is just down the hall. Melody made Jondoe promise not to bother me.

But I didn't promise not to bother him.

I'm overcome by the urge to head to the kitchen to make the noisiest cup of tea ever. This isn't so hard to do. I open and close every cabinet to find a tea bag, then reopen and shut every cabinet to find a mug, and a third time to find the kettle. Not all this opening and shutting is entirely necessary.

And yet it is.

I'm at the sink filling the kettle with water when the hair on the back of my neck prickles. It's both chilling and thrilling, a whole new sensation without the braid.

I take a deep breath, turn around.

"Would you like a mug of tea?"

Jondoe nods dumbly, looking as awed by me as I am by him.

I open up the cabinet, take out a mug. My hand is shaking so much, I'm afraid I might drop it.

"You're glowing!" he says all at once, taking me by surprise.

"What?"

Jondoe blushes deep red, like a winterberry.

"You're *more* than glowing. You're . . . you're . . ."

"Fat?" I suggest.

"No!" He blinks a few times and his eyes flicker back and forth as he scans the MiNet for the right word. "Luminous! Radiant! Incandescent!"

I try not to yield to such flatteries so quickly. But the truth is, I'm unused to hearing them. Ram has never been one to wax poetic about my loveliness. And though Melody says I've been ranked on the MiNet as one of the all-time most beautiful mothers-to-be, the Church Council has forbidden me from reading any of my own media, lest I succumb to the sin of pride.

Jondoe braces himself on the countertop, keeping himself at a distance.

"Are you gonna catch hell from Melody for talking to me?"

Catch hell. That's an interesting way to put it. I know

it's just an ordinary expression, and he only means it as such. And yet there was a time in both of our lives that we believed hell *was* contagious, that it really was something you could catch in the literal sense, like the very Virus that threatens to end us all. Or rather, there was a time in *my* life I believed that. I don't know what Jondoe's religious beliefs really were before he met me; I only know what he claimed to believe. And I don't know what he believes now either. Melody keeps saying that he wants to be on the right path and is only pretending to be her boyfriend because he wants to do right by me. His pursuit of this "serious relationship" with my sister was also the only reasonable explanation he could give the media for his early retirement as a RePro.

"Since your night together, his heart just isn't into his job," Melody said when she asked permission to peruse her fake relationship with Jondoe. "He can't perform anymore because he can't stop thinking about *you*. He'd tell you this himself, and apologize for hurting you, if only you'd let him."

That's an apology I vowed to never allow myself to hear.

As a trained RePro herself, Melody should've already known that the heart doesn't have anything to do with the mechanics of his profession. (Then again, she's still a virgin, so I suppose that makes me more of an expert in such matters.) I told her that she and Jondoe could do whatever they liked, they could even start a real relationship for all

I cared because I was a married woman who was only looking to build a promising future for her family-in-the-making. She didn't believe a word of what I said.

As unconvincing as I was then, the opposite is true now. I've got that indomitable feeling in my bones again, like I'll be called upon to conquer. And soon.

"I'm tired of all the lies," I say. "I still believe in sin. And lying is one I don't enjoy committing."

Jondoe doesn't take the bait. He doesn't ask what sins I *do* enjoy committing. He asks another question instead.

"Is that why you ran tonight? Because you're tired of lying? Because you want to finally acknowledge the truth about . . ."

He can't bring himself to say it. So I do.

"About *our* twins?"

Jondoe brings his hands to his chest and closes his eyes at this, the first and only time I've acknowledged out loud what we've both known all along: These babies are his.

melody
harmony

IT'S ZEN, RIGHT HERE AND NOW, WAVING A CHEERY HELLO
from my bed.

"GAHHHHHHH! What are you doing here?"

"I'm sorry! I didn't mean to scare you!"

I'm totally naked! In my efforts to clutch my towel to
cover all my breedy bits, I fumble it to the floor. Gah! I'm
even clumsy like a real pregger! What's happened to me?

"Close your eyes, perv!"

This towel is for seriously inadequate for my substantial
square footage of skin. I might as well try to cover up with
a Cheerclone's micro-miniskirt.

"I didn't see anything! I swear!" he lies.

"Keep them shut until I tell you!"

I fumble around in my drawers for underwear, maxed

out MyTurnTee, and baggy drawstring pants. Only when I'm fully covered from neck to ankle do I give him permission to open up.

"You are so beautiful."

My wet hair is plastered to my face and I'm wearing an outfit that would have no problem getting the purity seal of approval from the Goodside Church Council.

"Stop mocking me."

"I'm not mocking you!"

"This is beyond stalky, Zen. Even for you. What are you doing here?" And though I know I shouldn't, I keep talking. "The last I saw of you, you had your, um . . ." I tremble in memory of Ventura's viper tongue. "Mouth full."

Zen shakes his head, looking contrite.

"I'm here to tell you that was a mistake," he says. "I was being stupid and I'm sorry and I couldn't wait until tomorrow to tell you."

"Where's she now?" I ask, knowing I sound like a brat and not caring.

"Home, I guess," he says. "I don't know."

He pats the bed to encourage me to sit beside him. I do, but mostly because I'm practically asleep on my feet and it would take more energy to argue standing up.

"Is that why you're here? So you could own up to your stupidity and apologize?"

"Yes," he says, "and no. There's more to it than that."

With Zen, there's always more to it than that.

He sits up purposefully, cradles my cheeks with his hands. Then he does what I've been desperate for him to do since the first and only time we kissed.

He kisses me again.

harmony
melody

JONDOE IS SITTING AT THE KITCHEN COUNTER. I AM BUSYING myself with the kettle.

If anyone were lying in the grass in the dark, spying into our illuminated window from the outside, how easy it would be to mistake me for a good wife, noble of character and full with child, serving her husband after his day of hard but satisfying labor.

There's too much to say. And so much I long to do.

I wish I were wearing an apron so I could pocket my trembling hands.

"I don't want to get you in trouble with Melody," Jondoe says.

"I'm already in trouble," I say, nodding to my belly, "in case you hadn't noticed."

This makes him laugh. And I swear on a stack of Bibles that I could do without music for the rest of my life if only I could be surrounded by the sweet sound of Jondoe's laughter. It wouldn't be much of a sacrifice, not when I think of all the deprivations I've endured thus far.

In Goodside, I was raised to surrender my individuality and submit to the wisdom of the community. I was warned not to question the Council. Follow the Orders and earn my eternal reward. Defy the Orders and I'd suffer in a godless eternity. It was that simple. The Church boundaries—both physical and biblical—were there to ensure my safety and spiritual happiness. I learned that all Othersiders lived lives of unrestricted hedonism, and I lived in fear of all the sins I would inevitably sin if my free will wasn't kept in check by the Church's protective prohibitions. By blocking out all godless distractions, I would be a better believer.

But it hasn't worked that way.

When I snuck away to Otherside in the wee hours of my wedding night, I told myself that I was going there for Melody, because I was worried for her soul. I told myself that if I could persuade her to come back to Goodside with me, to follow in my spiritual path, I would *become* the person she needed to follow.

I was taught that sex was created for marriage and that it works best within that union. Why did it feel so wrong when I tried to lay down with Ram on my wedding night? Because I don't love Ram in that way and I never have.

I love—I *once* loved—Jondoe. I felt married to him in my heart, even without the vows. Even, as it turned out, if his intentions weren't true.

Jondoe sits and I stand, not knowing what to say, not knowing how to start, our audible breathing filling the silence.

"You cut off your braid," he says quickly.

"You hate how it looks, don't you?"

A slow smile spreads across Jondoe's face.

"It isn't about how you *look*, it's about who you *are*," he says. "Otherwise, I would have just as easily fallen for your twin."

I swallow the lump in my throat. It's a relief to hear it, this blunt articulation of my secret fear: that Jondoe would fall in love with my sister because he couldn't have me.

"But you didn't."

"I didn't."

"Why not?"

"Because she isn't you, Harmony."

Melody used to be the one so hung up on our indistinguishable genetics. If someone else could do her job exactly as well as she could, then what kind of value did she have? Now I'm the one who can't stop thinking about how easily Jondoe could swap one of us for the other and it wouldn't make the slightest difference to him.

"Harmony," he says in a halting voice.

I'm not ready to talk about everything we need to talk about.

"Was the costume your idea?" I ask.

Jondoe looks down at his suit. "I thought it would make me less conspicuous. Obviously it didn't work because I got caught."

He pinches his cheeks and chin, peels off the fake beard, and sets it down on the table. I want to press that beard to my own face. I turn toward the sink, grab the nearest rag, and press it to my mouth to fight this nonsensical urge. I inhale the cloth and take in the bracing scent of lemon cleaner to snap me back into my right mind.

"Then again, you're here and I'm here," Jondoe continues, sweeping his arms around the kitchen. "So I guess it *did* work."

"How did you get to Goodside?" I ask, my voice slightly muffled by the cloth.

"It was very special forces, secret ops."

I take another breath into the rag. In and out. Slowly. In and out.

"I commissioned a plasma plane and had it drop me off about a mile down the road. I was all stealth on foot the rest of the way, until I reached the gates. I wanted to avoid a hassle with security, so I crept along the perimeter looking for what I hoped was unguarded greenspace, then I scaled the fence . . ."

"You did?"

"I *am* in peak physical condition, Harmony, though it would have been better if I'd thought to wear my night-vision contacts. Even with my twenty-ten vision I had difficulty seeing in the dark and misjudged my footing."

I glance over my shoulder and watch as he holds up two palms still caked in dirt. And now that I look closer, I see that the knees of his pants are all muddy, and the pocket of his suit has almost torn away completely.

"Well, as you must know, there is no such thing as unguarded greenspace in Goodside."

No, not since I all-too-easily slipped away to Goodside the morning after my Honeymoon. That's when the Council posted Guardians to watch over the most vulnerable points of exit. And entry.

Jondoe continues his story. "I had barely recovered from my fall when I was looking down the barrel of a shotgun. I was captured by this skinny kid with a cracking voice." Jondoe screws up his face and starts squawking like a goose. "I GOT A TRESPASSER! I GOT A TRESPASSER!"

It's a dead-on impersonation of Zeke Yoder, and I laugh harder than I have in months. The laughter relieves the tension in the way the breathing rag could not. Oh my grace, it feels so good to laugh, even if it is wicked to do so at someone else's expense. Would Jondoe be surprised to hear that this "kid" is engaged to be married at the end of the month?

I find the confidence to turn around completely.

"He's Ram's closest friend. It must have been very exciting for him to spot you. We haven't had a security breach in many months."

Right after The Hotties went public, Othersiders became very, very interested in learning more about the Church. For weeks the Guardians were pulling their shotguns on one person after another who scaled the fence in the hopes of getting a picture of me milking a cow or clasping hands in prayerclique. Eventually, they gave up when they realized that I would only participate in prayerful media opportunities. I do believe the shotguns helped them accept this reality sooner than they might have otherwise.

"When I told Zeke I wanted to convert, I wasn't bluffing. I'm ready to change my ways. I've *been* ready, all this time. I was just waiting for the opportunity to tell you. I was waiting for *you*!"

"You're willing to trade in your fame?" I point to my belly. "For *this*?"

"For *you*."

"This is not a proper conversation," I say, trying to take the quaver out of my voice. I turn my back to him once more, and put far too much care and attention into selecting a flavor. "I am a married woman." My hand shakes as I reach for a tin of raspberry leaf tea.

"What do you think will happen to Ram, anyway?" Jondoe asks.

"I hope they give him a choice in the matter."

Ram loves any opportunity to go outside the gates. He loved arriving for parties early and leaving late—usually without me. Before he left tonight, I was tempted to remind him to be discreet when choosing his company, especially now that we've come this far. But I didn't say a word because I've come to believe that he has the right to spend his time with whomever he wishes. I've agreed not to acknowledge his secret, as he has so generously elected not to acknowledge mine. Mutual denial has brought us closer than ever and keeps our marriage—such as it is-alive.

"Look at me, Harmony. I'm a mess."

Ignoring the low wail of the kettle, I do as he asks. He's slumped over the table now, wearing a desperate hangdog look I've never seen before. Not even his luminous smile can lift him up.

He *is* a mess.

He's a bigger mess than I am. And *I'm* the adulteress here.

I take a step toward him and he rises from his stool at my approach. For a few seconds we just stand there, not talking, not touching, until I bravely reach out with a single finger and tug gently at his torn jacket pocket.

"You think you can fix me up?" he asks.

He's not referring to any mending that can be done with a needle and thread.

melody

ZEN IS KISSING ME AND I'M KISSING HIM BACK.

We are kissing. Oh my god. Zen and I are kissing.

OH MY GOD. WE ARE KISSING.

WE HAVE TO STOP KISSING.

"Stop!" I gasp, "We can't . . . we can't . . ."

We can't stop kissing. Our mouths have made their way to each other again. . . .

"We can't do this!" I shout, pushing Zen off me. How did we get horizontal so quickly? And in my condition?

"I disagree," Zen says, breathing heavily. "I think we can. And should." Then he takes my left hand and kisses it right between the third and fourth knuckles, and I swear there has never before been a more romantic gesture performed by a seventeen-year-old boy. Ever.

"I think it's time to use it," he whispers.

And even though I think I know what he means, I have to ask what he means, because what I think he means cannot possibly be what he means, because that would be OFF-THE-SPRING INSANE.

"Use what?"

"This."

And he holds up the padlocked condom and beams.

Oh, just terminate me now. That's what I thought he meant. Zen obviously has Sympathetic Gestational Psychosis. Which is even crazier than crazy, considering my bogus gestation.

"As our grandparents used to say," he says, shaking the padlock, "'no glove, no love.'"

"Glove? What's that have to do with it?"

"It's one of the slogans I thought we could reintroduce to the world as part of the Mission . . ."

The Mission. Always with the Mission.

"Gah, Zen! Dose down, already!" I exhale loudly. "I understand that this is all part of your grand vision and all, but what good are the slogans when that," I say, pointing to the padlocked box, "is one of the last condoms left in the country? Now, I'm no expert, but I'm pretty sure it's not, like, recyclable, right? I mean, you can't reuse it. . . ."

"No, I can't," he says. "But very soon I won't have to share. Don't you see how your big reveal could be the beginning of a reproduction revolution?"

I am way too tired to have this conversation right now.

But that's the thing about Zen. I just can't stop myself from getting tangled in his hypotheticals.

"Reproduction revolution? Isn't that going a bit too far? *Some* people have to procreate, Zen. Or the human race will—"

He starts laughing before I even finish.

"Go extinct? Ha! That's the greatest lie about the Virus."

I give him my blankest stare.

"Look, before the Virus, parents were totally neggy about their kids having sex. Like, if you had sex before marriage, you were definitely going to hell. And dads would take their daughters to these things called purity proms where they got all dressed up and the girls signed pledges saying that they would stay virgins until their future husbands got, like, written permission from daddy."

"Yeah, yeah, yeah," I say. "You seem to forget that adolescent oppression in the early to mid 2000s is one of Ash and Ty's favorite topics."

When my parents aren't coaching other parents in the science of "Breeding a Breeder" (their most popular seminar to date), there's nothing they enjoy more than going manifesto about their own sexually repressed youth.

"Abstinence only. Remember that ridiculousness?"

"Hahahahahahahaahaha . . ."

"Ooooh. Babies having babies . . ."

"It was a teen pregnancy epidemic, remember?"

"Right," Zen says. "So you know that if their generation

refused to heed the warnings and decided to do it anyway, they were told that they *had* to do it with a condom or else their penises would *fall off* and their wombs would *fall out*."

"Harsh," I say.

"Totally harsh. And guess what? It didn't stop everyone from having sex with and without protection. You've heard our president get all nostalgic about how we were number one in the world in teen pregnancy, right? Teens had every incentive NOT to pregg. They were shamed out of it. Scared out of it. And teens still did it in record numbers."

I was slowly catching on to his overall point.

"So you're saying that even if condoms were legalized and made available to the gen pop, there would *still* be enough couples doing it without them that the human race would be in no danger whatsoever of extinction?"

"Exactly."

This is so not what we were taught in school. It's hard to wrap my brain around it.

"So . . ." he says, sliding his hand up my leg. "Can you think of a more fun way to lead a revolution?"

harmony
melody

JONDOE LOOKS DOWN AT MY BULGING MIDSECTION, THEN UP AT
me. I answer his inquisitive expression with a nod. He
tentatively reaches out to place his hands on my belly and I
close my eyes in anticipation of his touch. . . .

"EEEEEEEEEEEEEEEEEE!"

The kettle screams.

I abruptly break away to remove the kettle from the
heat. *What am I doing?* I am a married woman! I made one
big mistake one night eight and a half months ago that
can't be undone now. But that's no reason to compound
that mistake with an even bigger one!

Turning my back to him isn't a solution. Fussing with
the tea can only keep me busy for so long. Eventually I will
have to turn around again and look straight into the face of

what I've been missing for the past eight and a half months.

No, what I've been missing my entire life.

The screeching kettle has woken up the twins, who are more rambunctious than ever after their brief rest. I pitch forward, clutch my underbelly, and try not to groan, but one escapes me anyway.

"Ooooh my graaaaace . . ."

"Are you okay?" Jondoe is right behind me now, a capable hand on each shoulder. "What's happening to you?"

"I'm fine," I say through gritted teeth. I take a few shallow breaths until the pains go away. "It's normal. The twins are just stretching out."

I right myself and rotate around just in time for one of the girls to ram her head right up against my stomach. Jondoe jumps backward, smashes into the countertop, and nearly topples to the floor.

"HOLY MOTHER. WAS THAT A *FACE*?"

My top is so tight that yes, one can actually see specific body parts as the twins are wrestling around in there. I've never seen a face before, but that's not to say that it's not possible.

Jondoe is paler than any veil I used to wear. "For serious. I think I saw a nose and a mouth. A FACE. That's the freakiest thing I've ever seen."

"You've never seen a pregnant woman's belly before?"

"Not a real one. Up close. Like that."

"How is that possible?"

He sighs. "My business is all about before and during. Not after."

I take a moment to let this sink in. Then he corrects himself again.

"Was," he says. "My business *was*. Because I'm not in the business anymore. I'm opting out. And not because I have to, either. I'm not shooting blanks or anything. I quit because I want to make this—us—work."

Isn't this exactly what Melody has been saying all along?

"Stop talking like this," I protest. "I'm married."

"But are you *really* married, Harmony? In the eyes of God?"

He has a point there. Ram and I have never . . . consummated. We've always been more like brother and sister than man and wife. Explaining our peculiar circumstances to the Church Council would require confessions that Ram and I are unwilling or unable to make.

I feel Jondoe's eyes on me and I can't return his gaze. When I look away, I catch sight of the canvas rucksack that Ram had given me. I'd left it on the counter and forgotten all about it. Jondoe notices it now too.

"What's in the bag?" he asks.

"I don't know."

Without asking, he scoops up and unzips the bag. He roots around for a few seconds before pulling out an electric razor and a box, which he hands over to me for closer inspection.

It's a package of hair dye in Basic Black.

And it brings tears to my eyes.

Ram had actually listened when I told him I wanted to shave off my hair and dye it black. And he wanted to help me do it. He went out of his way to buy it on the way to the party because he of all people understands my urge to be someone else. Dear Lord, I pray he's okay.

I channel the urge to cry in a more productive way.

"Is this meant for you?" Jondoe asks.

"Yes!"

I'm overcome by another rush of giddy energy that makes me want to do *something*.

"You really want to do this?" he asks.

I nod vigorously. I do.

Jondoe grins mischievously, rubs his hands together in anticipation, all at once shucking the hangdog and returning to the man I fell for all those months ago.

"Then let's do it."

melody
harmony

"LET'S DO IT," ZEN SAYS. "WHY NOT?"

"Why not?" I ask incredulously as I stand up. "Are you serious? With me looking like *this*?"

I do a slow, ungraceful twirl, making sure he takes in every lumpy inch of me. How can he possibly find me attractive?

"There are positions that are suited for your condition," Zen says, helpfully pantomiming one such position that resembles an isometrics exercise I used to do in soccer practice to strengthen my quadriceps. If *that's* sex, there is nothing sexy about it.

"Um, I don't think so, Zen."

"This can work, Mel. I've—"

If he finishes this sentence with the word "practiced,"

I will cut a cord right here and now.

"—*diagrammed* the whole thing, taking your new, um . . . physique into account."

"Wow, this is sounding sexier and sexier."

"I've calculated the premium positioning for maximum penetration. . . ."

"Stop talking."

". . . What goes where and how. . . ."

"Seriously. Stop talking. We've been through this a million times, Zen. I can't do it while I'm wearing this," I say, holding up the MOM bracelet. "If I take it off, the alarm will go off. And if I *get* off, the alarm with go off. So we're at an impasse here."

Zen smirks at me knowingly. "When's the last time your alarm went off?"

When I saw you and Ventura playing tonsil hockey.

"Why does that matter?"

"It matters," he insists. "When?"

"Right after I met the Jaydens," I lie. Part of me wants him to call me out on it, if only because it means that he wasn't so obliviated by Ventura's tongue that he didn't hear the alarm go off.

"We were getting pretty hot and heavy before, weren't we?"

Cheeks burn bright just thinking about it. "Yeah? So?"

"Your adrenals were pumping away," he says, like he's giving me a hint. "Your heart rate increased, your blood vessels contracted. . . ."

He stops talking and just stands there smirking at me. Has he always smirked so much? Or is this Ventura's influence?

After a few moments of smug silence, the truth hits me. "No!"

"Yes!"

"Please tell me you did not hack into and deactivate my alarm!"

"I can't tell you that."

"Zen! That can get you—get *us*—in major trouble. Messing with MOM is a national offense! Isn't the Mission enough to get us into trouble already?"

Zen stands up and plants himself right in front of me. "I don't care anymore!"

"You don't care?"

"I. DON'T. CARE."

He's got his determined face on, the one he wears against his opponents, be it in Ping-Pong or debate. The one that says he won't back down until he's victorious.

I do not like the idea of being something he has to conquer.

"How can you not care? When we came up with The Hotties, we agreed that we were *all* in this together. I don't understand why you would want to blow it when we're so close to making the Mission a reality. I thought the cause meant everything to you."

He looks up at me with sad eyes. "Not everything."

There's a bit of a gap between my IQ and EQ, so it

takes me a moment to figure out what he's talking about.

Me. I'm the everything.

"But I'll still be here when it's all over, Zen. I'll still be me. And we *can finally unburden ourselves of our virginity together.*"

I say this part like, way overdramatically, so it seems like I'm taking it less seriously than I really do.

"But not now, Zen, not like this. . . ."

"Why not *now*?" He looks at me with something like desperation. "Why not like this? How you look doesn't matter to me."

He keeps tugging on his hair spikes and is bouncing his knees up and down so rapidly that the whole bed is vibrating.

"Are you high?" I ask him.

"No! I'm just . . . ready. Really, really, really ready to do it. Is that so wrong? I want to use this while I still can!"

No one can break through when Zen is going full-on manifesto. Before I can stop him he punches the padlock, removes the condom from its box, and tears open the square foil package.

When he examines the contents, his crazed grin disappears.

"What? Can I see?"

I've never seen a condom out of its wrapper, but I'm afraid Zen might mistake my scientific interest for interest of an altogether different kind.

"Mutherhumper," he mutters. He tips open the package

and a small pile of brownish dust collects in his palm.

This is not what I was expecting. I don't know exactly what I was expecting, but that definitely wasn't it. Zen laughs in a cheerless way, gets up, and brushes the dust into the nearest trash bin.

I gasp. "That was one of the last condoms left in the country!"

"No," Zen replies flatly, rubbing the last bit of residue off his hands. "That's what happens to one of the last condoms in the country when it's improperly stored for more than a decade."

Zen sits back down on my bed, his head in his hands. Crushed.

"I want to do it with you. I've *always* wanted to do it with you."

"But why the emergency? Why right n—?"

And before the question leaves my mouth, it hits me.

I look at Zen and he looks back at me guiltily. We silently share this new bit of information as swiftly as a MiChat, only our exchange is totally no-tech.

Something *could* happen between Zen and Ventura. And I'm not talking just physically, but like, *emotionally*.

Which is way, way worse.

harmony

melody

I'M PERCHED ON A STOOL IN MELODY'S PARENTS' BATHTUB with a shower cap on my head. Jondoe is blasting my scalp with the hair dryer. It's impossible to talk over the whooshing air, which is probably better right now anyway because there's still too much to say and I have no idea where to start.

He turns off the dryer but my head still feels like it's smoldering.

"That's normal," Jondoe assures me. "That's how you know the color activation process is . . . um . . . activated."

"Oh," I say. Part of me wishes he would turn the hair dryer back on again to ease the burden of conversation.

I remove the cap and shake out my dry, freshly dyed hair with my fingers.

Jondoe is agog.

"You hate it," I say.

"On the contrary," he says, "I'm just surprised how the darker color suits you. It's like you were a brunette trapped in a blonde's body all this time."

I have a quiet laugh at this. I've spent my whole life feeling trapped, but hair color does not rank high on my list of oppressors.

"You still want to go short?" Jondoe asks.

I nod.

"I'll have to cut it down with scissors before you use the shaver. . . ."

"*I'll* have to cut it down," I say. "I'm doing this. Not you."

I had also insisted on applying the dye all by myself with him hovering over me, coaching me through it. It wasn't merely a matter of propriety. It's important for me to be in control of my destiny, even if it's just my hair at stake. Plus the task at hand required my full concentration, so all conversations were put on hold.

"I've done business with so many actresses and models—" He stops short, slaps his hand over his mouth. "What I mean is, I have a lot of experience." He grimaces and corrects himself again. "*Styling* experience! I have a lot of styling experience, you know, from all those photo shoots and spending so many hours with the fashion elite. . . ."

Jondoe is mistaken if he thinks any reminder of his past will convince me that he's in no way ready to repent. He seems to be forgetting that the worst sinners always have the *best* testimonies, that the most powerful conversion stories are told by those who had the hardest and longest journey from sin to redemption. Every time he hints at the man he used to be, he serves as a reminder of the person he has become.

I know this from personal experience. I've recounted my own fall from grace many, many times over for the congregations and prayercliques all over the world who have made the minimum donation to hear the holy half of The Hotties witness to them via the MiVu about nearly losing her soul to Satan's temptations in Otherside. Of course, the version I deliver to the true believers omits the very worst of my sins. Though when I let myself plunge the depths of Jondoe's eyes, I can't stop myself from thinking that lying down with him was the *best* of my sins.

Dear God. Why do you lay these feelings in my heart?

I pick up the scissors from the rim of the tub, grab hold of a clump of hair right in front, and hack away at it carelessly. Jondoe flinches at my lack of technique. What's happening on my head is definitely not pretty. But I think that might be the point.

Jondoe opens his mouth to make a suggestion.

"When I need your help," I say, "I'll ask for it."

He shuts his mouth. Closed.

For the next few minutes, I just cut and cut and cut with the scissors. I don't even glance at the mirror, I just feel my way around. Feathery black tendrils fall down all around me and scatter around the inside of the bathtub.

"If you want it shorter than that, you should probably switch to the electric razor," Jondoe says tentatively. "How short do you want it anyway?"

"Short," I say, pinching a clump of hair at my crown.

"Okay." He comes closer to investigate. "That's about two inches."

Jondoe places the correct attachment over the teeth of the razor and hands it over.

"Are you sure?" he asks.

"I'm sure."

When I press the razor against my scalp, the buzziness shoots straight from my head and electrifies my entire body. When the twins respond accordingly, I have to brace myself on the edge of the tub.

"Are you sure you're okay?" Jondoe asks.

I bite my lip and nod, fighting against this latest wave of pain.

"Can I help you?" he asks. "With the parts you can't reach?"

I know he's really talking about my hair. But this time I wish he weren't just talking about my hair.

"You may," I reply. Though what I'm really thinking is, *You already have.*

Jondoe rests his hand on the nape of my neck and oh my grace. He's making miracles with his fingertips. His touch makes everything melt way. I feel like I've been unburdened of my physical body, my soul promoted to glory. I close my eyes and surrender . . . surrender . . . surrender . . .

"Harmony?"

I don't know how long ago he finished. He's set the shaver down and stepped backward to take me in. His eyes are wide, his mouth agape.

"Do you want to see what I see?" he asks.

"I do."

He steps to the side to unblock my view of the mirror.

"Oh my—"

I'm looking at the most startlingly pretty girl I've ever seen.

He cropped my hair as short as I had asked him to, except in the front, where it falls down in longer, jagged slices across my forehead. My eyes seem bigger and more indigo than blue. My nose and mouth aren't as delicate as before, but more dramatic. Striking. Strong. I don't look anything like the fragile flower I've been told I was my whole life.

I don't look anything like my twin, either.

"I haven't spent much time around preggers," Jondoe

says, "but you have to be the most beautifully bumped girl that has ever been."

"You did a praiseworthy job," I say. "Thank you."

He reaches around and unfastens the buttons on the cape draped around my shoulders and removes it with a showy flourish, scattering hair all around the tub. Then he makes a grand gesture out of taking my hand and helping me step up and out of the tub. I know I'm still carrying an extra forty pounds, but I feel lighter than air. It's not just Jondoe's presence and attention, either. I can't stop touching my neck, my ears, my collarbone; it's like I've never seen these parts of myself before. I'm totally exposed, and yet at the same time, I feel safely hidden behind a new identity. Will anyone even recognize me like this if I don't even recognize myself?

I'm stroking my wispy sideburns with my fingertips when he comes up on me from behind and bends down to whisper in my ear.

"Let me sleep beside you tonight."

Each word is like a caress to the most tender skin on the back of my neck.

I shiver, wanting the impossible. Wanting *more*.

He knows this too. After his many years in the business of making—and faking—love, it would be impossible for him not to.

"Chastely!" he adds hastily.

It's not supposed to be funny, but it is.

"Ha!" I point to my swollen midsection. "As if there's a choice in the matter!"

There's a moment's pause.

Then Jondoe and I share a long laugh that is simultaneously the most natural and most miraculous sound I've ever heard.

THIRD

"For where your treasure is, there your heart will be also."

—Matthew 6:21

harmony

"EEEEEEEEEEEEEEEEEE!"

This time the screeching isn't coming from the kettle. It's me.

Jondoe flails around from his spot on the floor next to the bed.

"WHAT DID I TELL YOU? NO ALARMS! EVER!"

"Why . . . are . . . you . . . yelling . . . at . . . me?" I ask, taking a breath in between each word.

Jondoe turns and stares at me like he's startled to be here.

"Oh, Harmony, I'm sorry," Jondoe says. "I thought you were Moxie."

"Who . . . is . . . Moxie?"

"My personal assistant." He groans, then vigorously rubs

the sleep out of his eyes. "I thought she set an alarm. And I have told her time and again that there are to be no interruptions of my circadian sleep cycle because it can be really bad for reproductive circulation. My biorhythmist recommends that I wake up naturally every day because it increases blood flow to, you know, my most vital extremity. . . ."

The twins settle down, the pain fades away, and I sink back into the pillows.

"So was that *you*? *Screaming?*"

I nod weakly. It felt like the twins were trying to escape through my belly button, but I don't want him to know that.

"I'm fine now."

Jondoe's eyes bulge. He extends his arms in front of him and pantomimes my belly.

"Did you double in size last night?"

It sure looks that way, as if the twins are jockeying for lead position.

"You think . . ." He points wordlessly at my stomach.

He's thinking what I'm thinking. But I'm not ready to say it out loud.

Jondoe leaps to his feet and claps his hands together.

"I can do this!" he announces. "You'll see, Harmony! I won't disappoint you!"

And before I can ask what he's doing, he's already run out of the room, leaving me alone and in fear of the next shockwave of contractions.

melody
harmony

harmony

BEEP! BEEP! BEEEEP!

At first I think it's MOM. But then I remember: Zen deactivated my alarm.

But I don't have time to think about him because the beeping isn't coming from my own wrist, it's coming from my driveway. It's the Bumpmobile! Ready to take me to school! I've overslept! And I've got a biochem exam today!

My friends make fun of me for studying so hard when I've made enough money to afford the luxury of never having to bust another brain cell. But I actually like learning stuff. I mean, how cool would it be if I discovered a cure for the Virus? Or if not a cure, how about the invention of an artificial method that actually works? Billion

Dollar Hottie Saves the Human Race. How's that for a narrative arc?

Okay. And maybe I also need to go to school to fix the mess that I made last night.

BEEEEP! BEEEP! BEEEEEEP!

The Bumpmobile's horn is notoriously obnoxious. We call it the waterbreaker.

I rush around the room, getting ready as quickly as I can with all this extra poundage. Even though I know the Bumpmobile would never leave without me, I've worked too hard to maintain my everygirl image to get all diva now. So I twist my hair into a ponytail and pull on a MyTurnTee and pair of stretch jeans. I splash cold water on my face, and make sure to squeeze a good-sized splurt of toothpaste out of the tube and directly into my mouth. I don't really care what I look like today—and to be honest, I know I can pull off the fresh-out-of-bed look pretty well—but I don't need the entire MiNet buzzing about my death breath.

BEEEEEEP! BEEEEEEP! BEEEEEEEEP!

I'm only half awake, so I almost speed-waddle right past Jondoe in the kitchen. He's filling the kettle with water.

"Melody!" he says, "I was just about to wake you—"

"I'm late for school," I interrupt in a rush. "You're finally going to get that time alone with Harmony that you've wanted for so long."

Jondoe looks confused for a moment, then brightens as if he's suddenly remembered something.

"Don't worry about us!" he says, settling the kettle on the burner. "I know what I'm doing!"

I know that voice. It's the same one he uses to shill E-REX energy drinks. I can't help but think he's trying to convince himself more than me.

"Just take it easy on her, okay? I'll be home by three-fifteen at the latest!"

With a twinge of reservation, I grab my knapsack and a blueberry PregGo Bar and meet the Bumpmobile barely two minutes after the first *BEEP*.

harmony
melody

JONDOE RACES BACK INTO THE ROOM.

"Boiled water? Check." He marks the air with his finger.

"What?"

"The water is boiling! You can't have a baby without boiled water? Right? And clean sheets. We need clean sheets!"

This would be a very sweet gesture if I wasn't so worried about being split in two.

"I'm not having these babies here and now," I say. "We'll need to get to a birth center. My sister will know where to go."

Jondoe grimaces slightly. "Um . . . Your sister just left for school."

"She *left* me here with you?"

He puffs his chest up with pride.

"She trusted me enough to leave you in my care! She knows I've done my research! I've been studying up on how to be a perfect birthcoach. Go ahead, ask me anything! Ask me how many centimeters you need to be dilated before you can deliver!" He's too excited to wait for the answer. "Ten! See? I know what I'm doing!"

I want to make sure I'm hearing what I'm hearing.

"You did all this research for your job?"

"I did all this research for *you*." He looks away, suddenly shy.

"For me?"

"With the hope that I'd get to be with you when you deliver and coach you through it. And I will be!"

I barely have time to understand the full meaning of this before he's at my side, two fingers pressed to the inside of my wrist.

"Your pulse is strong," he says in a commanding tone. "How far apart are your contractions?"

"It's difficult to tell," I reply with uncertainty. "They seem to be coming pretty irregularly."

"Hmm . . ." he says, stroking his chin. "Could be a false alarm. Braxton Hicks. Your membranes didn't rupture yet, did they?"

"My *what*?"

"That's the technical term for asking, 'Did your water break?'"

Oh. I shake my head no. I can't get over how knowledgeable Jondoe is about birthing. He knows more than any man in Goodside, that's for sure. And he learned it all for me?

"Let's get you up and walking around," he says, reaching out to help me out of the bed. "If you're really ready to go, gravity will help move things along."

When I grab hold of him, I'm struck by emotions altogether different than the carnal stirrings of the past.

I feel comfort in his strong, capable hands.

melody

EVERYONE SMILES AT ME AS I CLIMB ABOARD. TO THESE GIRLS,
pros and amateurs alike, I really can do no wrong.

"I'm sorry for making you wait, everyone," I say, head-
ing down the aisle to my seat. "I overslept."

Throughout most of my fake pregnancy, I was perfectly
capable of riding my bike to school as usual. Even when I
wasn't showing, I had to take the Bumpmobile because *not*
taking it to school would have provoked elitist accusations.
These days, however, with forty pounds' worth of fake
babies sinking deep into my breedy bits, a mile would feel
like a marathon. So I'm relieved to have the ride, even if it
means I have to feign enthusiasm for all things preggy for
five minutes every morning and afternoon. On the upside,
it's one place I'm guaranteed not to run into Ventura Vida,

which is especially vital for my sanity after last night.

Being by greeted by a busload of knocked up Cheer-clones is only marginally better.

"Oh. My. Behbeh," squeaks Dea Lan, the squeakiest of the bunch. "I was totally there at your launch party last night! Don't believe me? Just take a whiff!" She shoves her wrist under my nose. "It's You: The Fragrance! So yummy! But are you, like, okay?"

As she asks this, she's already scrambling her own hair with her fingers and twisting it into a mangy ponytail that sticks out from the side of her head.

Dea bumped with a Baller named Asif at a masSEX-tinction orgy only a few days before I got mocked up, so she's been obsessively comparing herself to me, and copying everything I do along the way. Never mind that I'm supposed to be carrying twins and she's only got one oven-bunny wrecking havoc with her waistline.

Imitation comes naturally to Dea and all Cheerclones because they are experts in losing their individuality for the benefit of the collective. Each member is contractu-ally obligated to adjust her weight and dye her hair, eye, and skin color to duplicate the average for the group as a whole. While on their "gestational hiatus" from cheering, it's not surprising that Dea and the rest of the squad have redirected those talents toward morphing into me. Within thirty seconds nearly *every* girl on the Bumpmobile has copied my bedheadish look. And thanks to the MiFotos these girls snapped of me when I climbed aboard, I know this unattractive trend is already going viral on the MiNet. This morning busloads of girls all across the world will disembark from their vehicles with deranged side ponytails.

Celine Lichtblau is about the only one on the bus who hasn't adopted my hairstyle. She's too stoned to notice I've taken the seat across the aisle from her.

"Hey, Celine," I say, wincing at her waistline. "I'm surprised to see you here."

Celine, it should be noted, is practically ten months pregnant. I thought for sure she was supposed to be induced over the weekend.

She responds in slow motion. "Ohhhh . . . what?" Her eyes are red and glassy. "Weren't you supposed to go for a pop and drop on Saturday?"

She stares at me blankly for at least ten seconds. Then she covers her mouth and starts giggling uncontrollably.

"Ohhhh . . . yeah . . . I think I missed it," she says airily.

Every pregger gets prescribed AntiTocin so we don't bond with our bumps. But for the first trimester Celine was prescribed too much and it was like a nonstop crazy-bitchfest. For serious. We all just kind of quietly put up with her moods because we were afraid of her. Then one day she got an unfavorable grade on an essay titled, "Babies: What's the Big Fucking Deal?" and she flew into an epic hormonal rage and threatened to impregnate the entire Princeton Day Academy faculty with her fist. The made no sense but terrified our teachers and administrators nonetheless. After that incident, her OB kept her on the AntiTocin but hoped to lessen its psychotic effects by writing her a scrip for Mellonin, which she tokes via a smokeless vaporizer pipe. The combination of these two meds has certainly worked because she's pretty much down to just one mood: munchie.

"Heeeey . . . Do you have any . . . like . . . snickity-snacks? I haven't eaten . . . like . . . all morning and I'm *starving*."

There's a crumpled bag of Cheezy Chipz on the floor at her feet. Her mouth and fingers are tinged orange, and crumbs have settled on her coat and seat.

"All morning?" I ask.

"*All morning*," she replies with such dumb sincerity that I'm starting to believe that *she* believes she's telling the truth.

Her pregg is now just one of the many things in life she just can't be bothered with anymore, a list that includes just about everything but a) getting her next hit, and b) getting snickity-snacks. She's failing all of her classes, and the only reason she hasn't been bounced out is because of the recent passage of the Maternal Anti-Discrimination Education Act, which basically says that preggers (according to the quikiwiki) "cannot be punished academically for their invaluable role in the repopulation of our great nation." So it doesn't matter if a pregger is experiencing hormonally induced stupidity, is artificially dosed into stupidity, or is just naturally stupid with or without the human squatting in her uterus; she can get her diploma without testing proficiently in *any* of the subjects she's taken in four years of high school. And this policy will stop us from slipping into second-world status *how* exactly?

Sigh. That's a talking point straight from the Mission.

Fortunately, I get a MiNet message just in time to stop me from thinking about what I don't want to think about. I'm beyond amped when see that it's my friend Shoko calling me from college!

"Your hair is for seriously janked. You know that, right?"

That's why I love Shoko. She's the only one who doesn't treat me any differently since I got branded. I take my hair out of its sloppy side ponytail and smooth it over my shoulders. I try to ignore the fact that Dea and the rest of the Cheerclones are silently copying me.

"And you, Miss Weiss, are looking as diva as ever."

It's almost impossible to believe that this teeny pixie chick with the big mouth could have carried another human being inside her. Twice. Shoko just started her second semester at Rutgers and has recently pledged Eta Omicron Tau, the sorority with the reputation for having the hottest girls who "snapped back" after their deliveries. All of this was made possible with the money Shoko earned by providing two kids for a couple she never even met.

That's *exactly* the way Pro transactions are supposed to go down.

Well, minus the part when she almost died.

Shoko nearly bled out after her second delivery and had to get an emergency hysterectomy. She was so high on Humerall that she was more concerned about the ragged state of her cuticles than her near-death delivery. To be honest, she acted almost exactly like Celine does now. Shoko doesn't remember anything that happened in the OR and never caught sight of the human being she brought into the world that day.

"So did you and Jondoe break up or what?" she asks, getting straight to the point. "Because there's a nubie-pubie all over the MiNet saying that you did. And disgracing our PDA team jersey while doing it, I might add!"

Quailey. Gah.

"I thought I was your best friend! You promised not to lie to me anymore!"

Though she doesn't know the sketchy extent of our scamming, Shoko is the only outsider who has so much as a clue that The Hotties are not what we appear to be. Way back when this all started, I told Shoko that it wasn't *me* making major media with Jondoe, but Harmony pretending to be me. So she thinks Jondoe has bumped *both* of us, a position in keeping with her opinion that he is (in her words) "the stiffiest RePro in the business."

"We didn't break up," I say, which isn't a lie because you can't break up if you were never together in the first place. "I swear. She's just fame-gaming that's all."

Skoko wrinkles her nose the way she does when she detects bullshit.

"You swear there isn't something you're not telling me?"

There have been times that I've been so weighed down by this secret that I've come close to confessing to Shoko all about the B$B. She's always been brutally honest, and I know she would have given me a colorfully candid assessment of our scam:

"Did you get cock-knocked in the head? You're never going to get away with this!"

Yeah, that's *exactly* why I haven't confided in her. I don't want a confirmation of what I already know.

"I swear."

I've lied about a billion times in the past eight and a half months, and I swear it hasn't gotten any easier. But I don't get to see Shoko's response because my MiNet reception goes blind when the Bumpmobile pulls into the school parking lot.

These mornings are when I miss Shoko the most.

Malia too.

Malia is being treated for postpartum psychosis at the Shields Center. She's been there since last spring, when she tried to kill herself after she was told that she couldn't keep her "baby" (yes, she used the b-word) because it had already been picked up by the couple who paid for it. Surely she should be cured by now, right? She used to message me all the time about how it wasn't too late to save myself from preggsploitation, but I haven't had any contact with her since I went public with The Hotties. She probably thinks

I'm the ultimate sellout and has lost all respect for me. I hope she'll forgive me when I reveal the whole truth.

I hope *everyone* forgives me. Even if they don't agree with me.

Celine pokes my arm and gives me another one of her unreadable stares.

"For serious . . . Do you have any . . . like . . . snickity-snacks?"

I offer my PregGo Bar and she declines because they taste like sweaty shin guards. I'm only carrying it around with me because I'm paid to do so. No one seems to notice or care that I've never been seen actually eating one.

It's just another prop in this elaborate scam that has become my life.

harmony
melody

I'M PANTING LIKE A DOG IN A DROUGHT.

"Another contraction!" Jondoe says excitedly. "That's only five minutes after the last round! We should call an air taxi now!"

"No!" I insist, gripping the wall as I inch myself forward. "Not yet!"

"But you said yourself you don't want to deliver the twins here."

I don't want to deliver the twins here.

Or anywhere.

"It's too soon! I'm five weeks early!"

"Preterm labor is not uncommon with twins," Jondoe says assertively.

"How can you be sure I'm in labor?" I ask, panic rising

in my voice. "How do you know I'm not having those, um, Brixton Hacks—"

"Braxton Hicks," he corrects.

"WHATEVER!" I roar. "YOU ARE NOT A DOCTOR."

I've never raised my voice like that in my life. If I yelled at Ram like that, he'd scurry away with his puppy tail between his legs. But Jondoe doesn't back away. He stops and gingerly places his hand on the curve of my back.

"Exactly," he says softly. "Which is why we should go to a hospital."

I ignore his words, though his soothing touch is harder to resist. I'm determined to do a few more laps up and down this hall.

"The twins will settle down," I say unconvincingly, "this is a false alarm and—"

I stop midsentence.

Something has just happened inside me.

A pop. A pulling apart. A loosening. And releasing . . . releasing . . . releasing . . .

Within a minute, I'm soaked from the waist down.

"Ack! Gack! Ack! Gack!" I'm flapping around the hall like a goose with a broken wing. "The twins can't come now! I've got five weeks to go! It isn't time!"

"They can and they are," Jondoe replies, taking deep breaths to remain calm.

He offers his hands to me, but I take a step backward.

I'm scared to let him touch me. Afraid of what else might come apart.

He looks me directly in the eyes before speaking.

"Your water's already broken," he says gently. "There's nothing else I can break."

Oh, Jondoe. How I wish that were true.

melody

I NEVER THOUGHT I'D BE SUPPORTIVE OF THE CAMPUS-WIDE
MiNet blind, but the seven hours I'm in school are the
only part of my private life that stays private. No one can
foto me while I'm wearing my ugly protective goggles for
my biochem lab. No one can video me eating vitamin-
deficient snack products I am not being paid to eat. No
one can follow me into the bathroom and MiChat to all
my followers about how long and how often I pee.

But today I'm dreading a run-in with Ventura. I mean,
even more than the usual dread based on her usual annoy-
ingness. And I have no idea what I'll do when I see Zen.

I wish I could just sprint down the hall and hide out in
homeroom. But in my current state of maximum density, I
can't get anywhere nearly as fast as I need to. I don't know

how Harmony does it. She can still milk a cow or shovel manure, for Darwin's sake. My fake deliveries are making my whole body ache worse than the hardest, longest soccer practice I've ever had. Plus it doesn't help my progress when someone stops me every few steps to make one comment or another on the state of my uterus.

"You're bigger and better than ever!"

"Can I rub your belly for luck?"

"Work it! Flaunt it! You've got fattitude!"

I'm about halfway to my locker when I'm stopped by major gridlock.

"I'm trapped!"

"I'm staaaaaarving!"

Celine somehow jammed the steering mechanism on her Preggway and has pinned a defenseless pre-pubie freshboy against the vending machine. Preggways only go, like, a half-mile an hour, but Celine can't get through a day without a low-speed wreck. And we can't keep track of how many times she's lost her way, motored into an empty classroom, and was later discovered marveling at the pretty unicorns and rainbows projected from her hallucinogenic mind and onto the blank wall.

I'll say this about Celine: She's way more entertaining now than she was before she was dosing Mellonin.

Anyway, I always looked down on all the lazy bumpers who get their doctors to diagnose them with metatarsal edema (swollen ankles) just so they can get permission to motor through the halls. But by the time I reach my locker

I'm seriously considering getting a Preggway too because I'm ready to terminate myself. Especially when I see Zen has gotten there before me.

So. Yeah. I handled things pretty suckily last night.

But if there was a better strategy than locking myself in my bathroom and telling Zen I wasn't coming out until I knew he was gone, I still don't know what it is. Zen complied more quickly than I thought he would, and I can hardly blame him if he decided to head straight for Ventura's bedroom. I doubt he did though. Ventura is not discreet and news of their hookup would be all over the MiNet this morning.

Zen is leaning against my locker with his arms folded across his chest and one leg crossed over the other, the unnatural pose of someone straining very hard to look totally at ease. It's a relief, really, knowing that he feels as awkward about what happened—or *didn't* happen—as I do.

"Hey." His voice cracks. "Hey," he repeats in a baritone that I think is supposed to be sexy but has the opposite of its intended effect on me.

"Hey," I say back.

He runs a hand through his hair. I shift all my weight onto my right hip, trying to get comfortable.

"I kinda went about it all wrong last night, didn't I?"

"Kinda? It was a total fustercluck."

This makes him smile.

"You're right," he says. "And I'm sorry."

"I accept your apology."

Whew. That wasn't so awkward, was it?

Without anything to add, I punch the code to open the door.

Oh no.

"Surprise!" he says with a goofy flourish.

Inside my locker are a six-pack of Coke '99 and a box of chocolate chip energy bars.

"What's wrong? These are your favorites!" And then he proceeds to reach in, grab a bar, tear off the wrapper, and eat the whole bar in one big bite. "Mmm! Deeelicious."

"You're right. These are my favorites. And yours too, apparently."

Zen chews for a few seconds, then swallows. "Sorry, I didn't have time for breakfast," he mumbles.

"That's fine," I say, eyeing a smear of chocolate in the corner of his mouth.

"Then why are you making The Fuggy?"

He's right. I'm frowning and my forehead is furrowed. I make The Fuggy whenever I get too tired of hiding my true feelings, which is happening more and more the longer I'm mocked up.

I turn to him slowly, not to be dramatic but because that's the only speed I'm capable of achieving right now.

"Harmony told me that when Jondoe first came to my house, and he thought she was me, he tried to woo her— meaning *me*—by presenting her with the exact same gifts."

Zen's face falls. "What's your point?"

"My point is that *anyone* who takes a moment's glance at my file could know me just as well as you think you do. I've got a million MiNet followers who know me as well as you do."

And now, as an added measure of his distress, Zen pulls on his hair spikes.

"We've been naive to believe our relationship is any deeper than it really is."

Zen is shaking his head at me. "Don't do this, Mel."

"Do what? This is good news for both of us! It's so liberating!" I point to my ubiquitous face in an ad on the wall right behind Zen. "The National Association for Pro-creation didn't select me as their spokesteen without good reason! Why open our hearts and minds when we can open our files and legs!"

"Yeah, what she says!" says Asif, the Baller who pregged Dea. His locker is right next to mine and he's been graciously offering to bump hump me all year.

"Gah," I say to the Baller. "Delete yourself already."

Zen smiles uneasily. "Well, it's nice to know that you're rejecting *all* comers, not just me."

But Zen is the only one I struggle to resist.

He's licking his lips, not at all in a humpy way, but it's still having that effect on me anyway. As much as I want press my thumb to the corner of his mouth to wipe away that stubborn smudge of chocolate, I feel like I shouldn't touch him in that or any other way if he's so conflicted about what—who—he wants.

"Look," Zen says, quietly now, so we won't be overheard. "I don't know what you think *has* happened or *is* happening with me and—"

He stops himself before he says her name. I follow his wandering eyes behind me just in time to catch none other than Ventura herself hovering nearby. She unsuccessfully tries to escape detection by dashing into the boys' bathroom.

This, to me, is all the evidence I need that something has and is happening.

Mercifully, the last bell rings, putting an end to this conversation.

"I have to go now," I say. "Because I'm already too late."

harmony
melody

THE AIR TAXI HAS LANDED SILENTLY IN MELODY'S BACKYARD. And that's when I realize my escape plan has more holes than a pile of Ram's unmended socks.

"How do we know the pilot won't alert the media?" I ask.

"I have it covered," Jondoe says, gently stroking the worried wrinkle in my forehead. "There's no pilot. It's a preprogrammed droid. It's the only way I travel these days. How did you think we got here last night?"

I was so out of it last night that I hadn't even noticed.

We climb aboard and Jondoe helps extend the seatbelt to accommodate the vast acreage of my waistline. The air taxi lifts off and within what seems like seconds Melody's house is already in the distance.

"We'll be at the EBC in two minutes," he says.

I feel taken care of for the first time in far too long. The twins are settled down for now and I revel in this moment of relative calm. I need to reserve my strength for what lies ahead, and I pray we arrive before the next contraction.

"I'm sorry I wanked out when I saw the twin's face last night," Jondoe says. "All the research I've done didn't quite prepare me for that."

I can't blame him. I've had more than eight months to live with the idea and I still can't imagine what life will be like after the twins are born.

"I can't believe you had a plan all this time and you kept it to yourself," he says with admiration. "You're so encrypted!"

"What do you mean?"

"You didn't tell me or Melody or anyone!"

"Well, I didn't really have an escape plan in place. I—"

"Give yourself some credit, Harmony. Cutting and dying your hair was a genius way to disguise your identity! You don't want anyone to recognize you so you can deliver in Otherside without being stalked by the paparazzi! I only wish you had told me, though. I could have helped take your disguise to a whole 'nother level! With the help of some synthetic skinfeel, I could have given you a temporary racelift."

"A *what*?"

"You know, like for obsolescents who want to try on

165

their new raceface before committing to irreversible surgery. I could've turned you into a hundred-year-old Chinese man! I'm not sure why a hundred-year-old Chinese man would require admittance to a birthcenter, but that's beside the point. You would have been unrecognizable."

"But I didn't have a plan. . . ."

He waves my denials away with his hand. But the truth is, my makeover really wasn't as calculated as Jondoe is making it sound. I only knew that I wanted to try look like someone else for a while. But maybe, deep down, I *was* formulating this plan all along and it just wasn't until the Elders arrived on my doorstep last night that it all came together. That's when I finally realized that I wouldn't have *any* freedom of choice if I delivered in Goodside. If the Council voted for shunning, they would have taken the twins away. I reckon their new caregivers were already selected for me. Had one of the girls in my prayerclique already been assigned to the task, whether she knew it yet or not? The Council would've said this arrangement was for the good of the Church community. But would it have been good for the girls?

"I just want you to include me from now on, Harmony. Whatever it is, I'm in! I would have disguised myself by dying my hair too. But I guess this fake beard and hat will have to do."

I must still be frowning over the thought of the twins growing up with my housesisters because Jondoe squeezes my hand and offers a compassionate look.

"Oh, don't worry, Harmony," he says soothingly. "With my bone structure and complexion, I definitely could've pulled off the darker color." Jondoe runs his fingers through his wheat-blond locks. "Then again, so many wannabes have cloned my hair color that I could easily be mistaken for one of my handsomer followers."

Does he really believe I'm troubled about his *hair*? I heave a sigh.

"Were you this full of yourself when we met?"

Oh my grace. My mouth is as out of control as my body.

"Ha!" Jondoe barks in surprise.

"I'm sorry. That was unkind of me to say."

"No! Don't apologize!" Jondoe says. "You're right! I've played the famegame so long that I've forgotten what I was like before. It really warps your mind, being the object of the world's affection. I'm treated like everything I do or say is the awesomest thing that anyone has ever done or said, until the *next* thing I do or say becomes the awesomest. It's no wonder I started believing I was an instrument of God."

"You don't think you are?"

"I don't know what I believe anymore," he says with a hapless shrug. "But I'm working on it."

I nod in understanding.

"I've had a lot time to think about it, and I'm starting to believe that all that talk about me sowing the seeds of the Word was just a clever and convenient way to combine the two driving impulses in my life." He pauses, looks up to the Heavens. "God and sex."

My cheeks flush hotter than Hell itself.

Jondoe had been raised in an evangelical household that was about as religious as you can get in Otherside, though nowhere near as strict as my own. If he had grown up in a Church settlement, he would've been married by fourteen. Instead, that's the same age Jondoe convinced his parents that he was a uniquely gifted messenger of God, one who did his best missionary work in the missionary position, siring the next generation of true believers.

Like my twins.

"I want to change, Harmony, but it's hard. You're the only one who will tell me when I'm being a jackhole."

"My sister tells you."

"That's true," Jondoe admits. "But Melody doesn't like me either way, with or without the swagger."

"She likes you."

He rolls his eyes. "She *tolerates* me because of you," he says. "She's a great sister in that way. Speaking of Melody, I should have told her you were in labor. I guess I wanted to prove to you that I could provide all the support you need. That was a mistake. We should let her know we're on the way to the birthcenter, right?"

I've been praying on this all morning.

"If I tell Melody, she'll show up at the birthcenter with a swarm of media."

168

Jondoe thinks on this. "We could tell her to come in disguise. . . ."

"You know how bad she is with hair and makeup." I shake my head. "It's too risky."

"And what about your ma?" he asks. "Won't she want to know her daughter is delivering?"

I consider his question for a moment before answering, wanting to be both truthful yet fair to the woman who saved my life when she chose to adopt me almost seventeen years ago. As the sicklier, scrawnier twin, I might have foundered in an orphanage had it not been for the Church's openheartedness about taking in the neediest babies, the ones that no one else wanted.

The ones that—even now—no one wants.

"Harmony," Jondoe is saying now, trying to get my attention. "How can we get in touch with your ma?"

"Ma has many more pressing concerns," I decide.

"Are you *sure*?"

"Ma has helped raise forty-eight children, only eight of which she birthed herself," I say. "She has always loved me as she has loved us all. Equally, but economically."

I often used to wonder what it would be like to be an only child, the sole focus of my parents' love and affection. Would I have more easily believed Ma when she called me "a gift from God" if I hadn't heard her say the same exact thing in the same exact way to dozens of housesisters and brothers? Then I met Melody and saw how her parents have treated their only daughter more like a precious

169

commodity than a precious blessing.

God sure does like to do things on His own time, doesn't He? For all the many times I longed to be left alone as a child, it was only after I returned from Otherside with an appreciation for my parents and our sprawling house-family that He finally granted that particular prayer.

And if it weren't for Jondoe, I would be totally alone right now.

"Okay, Harmony, if that's the way you want it," he says in resignation. "But you are aware that we won't be able to hide behind our hair forever. Eventually people are going to figure out who we are." He strokes the wooly fake beard that successfully shields almost half of his face. "I mean, if one person gets a good look at my perfectly symmetrical abs, we're done for." He must think I'm about to chastise him again for his pridefulness because he quickly adds, "I'm *joking*. To lighten the mood."

I'll take him at his word.

"I know that," I say, "but . . . ohhhhhh . . ."

And the rest of that thought is lost to another round of contractions.

Of course I can't hide behind my new anonymity for-ever. Just long enough to figure out what I'm going to do about these babies.

When is God going lay *that* answer on my heart? I frequently recall what Ma taught me about "unanswered" prayers, and how they are God's way of telling me I'm not ready for His answer yet. The most prayerful way to behave in these situations is to be patient. To wait. But I've been patient for almost nine months! How much longer can I possibly wait, when these twins are already on their way?

The air taxi is descending now, targeting a landing pad in front of the Emergency Birthcenter, when Jondoe turns to me with a solemn expression on his face.

"What?" I ask, protectively clutching my belly as the air taxi touches down.

"I've messaged Ram," he says.

"How? Why?"

"How? The same way I always messaged you. By hacking the system. Zen taught me how to do it. And why? He's your husband. He should be here."

"But *you're* the one who questioned whether he was really my husband!" I sputter.

"I'm trying to do the right thing!" he exclaims. "To prove to you that I can be good!"

Where's this *conscience* coming from all of a sudden? But there's no time to talk about this now. An army of white-clad healthcarers is racing toward the air taxi. In seconds, I'm enveloped by a blur of white scrubs, white lights. There was once a time not too long ago when I might have mistaken them for angels readying me for the Rapture. I know lots of things now that I didn't know then. What will I know in the future that I don't know today?

"What's the status?" asks one of the healthcarers, a

woman with a trustworthy voice.

"I'm thirty-five weeks pregnant with twins and my water broke about fifteen minutes ago, and my contractions . . . ohhhhh . . ."

No words.

"I think they're coming every three minutes or so," Jondoe says.

I close my eyes and recoil in a private pain he will never experience or understand.

"Who's your doctor?"

I feel multiple hands help me out of the air taxi and lift me onto a rolling bed.

"We don't have one around here," Jondoe replies quickly. "We were . . . on vacation. She's five weeks early."

None of the healthcarers respond as if this is at all suspicious. I suppose this would only sound suspicious to someone who knows it isn't the truth. When I open my eyes I see that Jondoe is smiling with quivery lips. It's actually better that he's nervous because his megawatt grin would immediately give him away as the world-famous Reproductive Professional he is.

Or *was*.

"Preterm delivery is not uncommon with twins," the woman says, following alongside the bed as it rolls toward the entrance of the birthcenter.

"That's exactly what I told her!" Jondoe says.

With every bump and wobble I feel like the babies could just burst right out of me like a seedpod in springtime. I wish it were that easy. The Bible warns us about suffering pains in childbirth as punishment for Eve's Fall. And I've heard my housesisters' screams carry through open windows and across the settlement. I know what I'm in for. Melody tells me that most girls who deliver in Otherside are completely unconscious, but I want to be awake through it all. Eve isn't the only one whose sins need to be atoned for. It only seems just that I feel the pain of delivering these babies as intensely as I felt the pleasure in making them. The Bible promises I'll forget my anguish as soon as the babies are laid in my arms. But what if I don't want to forget?

"What's your name, honey?"

My name? I hadn't thought of a name! I don't even need to look to Jondoe for help.

"I'm Gabriel," Jondoe answers, "and this is . . . Mary."

Under these circumstances, is this a praiseworthy tribute to the Mother of God? Or pure blasphemy? I don't know what to think of Jondoe's intentions anymore. If I ever did. And why should I when he seems as conflicted and confuddled by his actions as I am?

"Well, I'm Grace, the birthnurse assigned to your case. . . ."

"Did you hear that, H—Mary?" Jondoe marvels. "Her name is *Grace! It's a sign from God!*"

Remarkably, Grace isn't flustered by Jondoe's thumpiness, even if I am.

I know he grew up that way, but it's not the side of him I'm used to seeing.

"You're in good hands here at Keystone Emergency Birthcenter," Grace says warmly as I'm wheeled through the doors and into the brightly lit hall of the birthcenter. She presses both hands onto my belly and gives me a reassuring look. "Now let's get you ready to bring two new little people into the world!"

With no disrespect to Grace, who is clearly a very professional healthcarer, I have my doubts that she'll be able to prepare me any better than God has.

Which is to say, not at all.

melody
harmony

I'M SITTING IN THE BLEACHERS, WATCHING LONGINGLY AS ALL
the boys and unbumped girls in my Personal Health and
Fitness class play Muggle Quidditch. I don't even like the
game very much, I think it's silly, but I so miss physical activity that I'd be thrilled if I could run around the
gymnasium with a broom between my legs, chasing after
the human snitch wearing a gold pinny. I miss being able
to *move*. Preseason training for soccer has already started
and I'm just about dying to get on the field with my team.
If Harmony pushes out the twins on time, I'll be able to
rejoin the team before our first scrimmage. I can't wait.

That's an ironic phrase: "I can't wait." I *can* wait. I *am*
waiting. All I do these days is wait.

"What did you get for number one?" asks Dea, who is

also sitting it out. Her hair falls over her left shoulder, just like mine.

I glance down at the for seriously wanked True or False quiz our teacher distributed to all of us sidelined preggers to pass the time while the rest of the class is at play.

1. Nine out of 10 girls who have NOT pregged by 18 regret their obsolescence.

"Really?" I say. "You need to ask? You have a fifty-percent chance of getting it right if you guess."

"Not all of us were blessed with your brainy DNA."

I flip over the paper and hold it up for her to see.

"And all the answers are on the back."

Answer: TRUE! Girls who have NOT helped in our nation's fight against sub-replacement population suffer from depression, cellulite, and bad hair days.

Dea checks this out for herself.

"Oh!" she says, slapping her hand to her forehead. "Duh!"

Duh is an understatement.

The National Association for Procreation provided almost all of the funding for our school's Personal Health & Fitness curriculum—we have them to thank for those sweet new Quidditch brooms—so it's not obvious why

NAP messaging is being disguised as a straightforward True or False test.

2. Fifty percent of girls pregg on the first try.
Answer: FALSE! Seventy-five percent of girls need to try multiple times before being bumped. Get an early start so you aren't a sad girl with a dimpled butt and split ends.

3. A dose of Tocin makes pregging painless—and possibly pleasurable—even with a less-than-perfect partner.
Answer: TRUE! So what are you waiting for?

I don't even bother turning in my test.

Instead I put it in my pocket to give to Zen later in the day, half hoping that this will help the Mission and will somehow make up for the awkwardness of last night and this morning. I'm so distracted by thoughts of our last two conversations that I don't even notice Ventura until I hear the clomping of her boots on the bleachers. She's coming right at me, boobs first. Without being told, Dea moves to the far side of the bleachers to get out of her way.

"We rilly need to talk." Ventura's mouth is tight. Not even a hint of a smirk.

"Do we?" I ask. *"Rilly?"*

She narrows her eyes but stands her ground.

"About what?" I ask, trying to sound casual.

"Not what," she says. "Whom."

I know it's grammatically correct, but gah. *Whom?* Who talks like that?

"Zen," she adds, as if her "whom" needed further clarification.

I rest my hands on my bump and try to do a better job of exuding coolness than Zen did at my locker this morning.

"What about him?"

She sits herself down right next to me, near enough that I can't help but inhale her scent, which is a totally calculated move on her part. Ventura always smells delicious because she douses herself in Get Him, the pheromone cologne scented with the essence of lavender and pumpkin pie. It's only supposed to have a seductive effect on guys, but I find myself fighting positive feelings for her whenever she's this close to me. I make an exaggerated show of sliding over on the bench to put some distance between us. She's not being subtle; why should I?

"I know what you two are up to," Ventura says matter-of-factly.

My back-of-the-neck hairs prickle. *She's bluffing*, I tell myself. *She knows nothing. Zen hasn't told her anything.*

Has he?

"I don't know what you're talking about."

Then suddenly, without any warning, Ventura presses both of her hands to my belly. I'm so shocked by the gesture that I don't even have the presence of mind to pull away. She's feeling for movement, and she'll get it, because the B$B is designed to respond to touch. Sure enough, when fake body parts rub up against her hands from the inside, she pulls them away. She looks down at her palms, then up at me.

And then, with absolute certainty, she says, "Those are not Jondoe's twins."

harmony
melody

I'VE BEEN WHEELED INTO A SMALL, STERILE-LOOKING ROOM. I'm connected to more complicated-looking medical equipment than I've ever seen before. The room resonates with *beeps*, *boops*, and *pings*, all generated from the two lives inside me.

Thumpthumpthumpthumpthumpthump . . .

I'm hypnotized by the sound of their synchronized heartbeats. To think that Melody and I were once so intimately joined.

Thumpthumpthumpthumpthumpthump . . .

I'm thinking about my birthmother again, wondering what it was like for her to deliver us. Did she already know she was going to leave us at the hospital? During our last brief and forbidden MiVu conversation I had asked Melody if she ever thought about the conditions that might have led to our birthmother's decision. And Melody—who has made it a policy not to subject herself to such ruminations—had surprised me by answering.

"With the names she gave us, she had to love music," Melody said with an uncharacteristically faraway look in her eyes. "And I bet she was around our age, not much older, like a sophomore or junior in high school. And her dream was to go away to college to study music. Maybe even an exceptional college, like Julliard. I like to think that she was one of those singer-songwriters who used to actually sing with her real voice and played guitar, not guitarbot, and way better than I ever will. I bet she was more like you in that way, and it's sweet that you're actually living up to your name, and then some."

I should have modestly insisted that I wasn't nearly as musical as Melody made me out to be, but I was too taken with the idea that I had somehow inherited talents from my birthmother that Melody had not.

"And she wrote heartbreaking songs about being misunderstood by wanky parents, brainless friends, and boys she loved who didn't love her back."

I was afraid to move so much as a single muscle. I wanted her to keep talking about our birthparents in a way that made them feel realer than the conjurings of my own heart and soul.

"Anyway, she knew she'd never be able to go away to college with two babies to take care of. So she did what she did." Melody had paused, closed her eyes for a moment, then continued. "The irony is, if Surrogetting was legal back then, she could have used us to help *pay* for school."

Melody failed to mention that we were both born with illegal toxins in our system. Our birthmother was probably not a driven, college-bound musical prodigy, and Melody knew it. She was spinning this perfect portrait of our birthmother not to preserve *her* own idealized image of the woman who delivered us, but mine. What harm would it do if she burnished our birthmother's image with fantastic figments of her own imaginings?

Like Melody, I too had always imagined that my birthmother was not much older than we are now. But I never believed that our birthmother was perfect. She had to have a troubled mind. Only someone so young and afraid would be driven to do what she did, to carry us for nine months only to leave us with strangers. And yet if she was so young, wouldn't she have had loved ones to turn to for help? The note attached to our blanket said, "Forgive me, Melody and Harmony." Not "us" but "me." That single word has haunted me for years. Why was she just "me"? Why was she alone? Where was her family?

Where is *my* family now?

Oh my grace. I've made another terrible mistake. Jondoe is right. Melody, of all people, should be here. She's the only true family I have. I want to tell Jondoe to contact her, but he's being asked questions by an intake nurse.

"You're the birthfather?"

"Yes!" Jondoe beams with pride.

Oh my! That famously radiant smile is going to get us into trouble! It's having an immediate affect on the intake nurse, who actually blushes and clutches a rubber-gloved hand to her chest. She's in swoon, but fortunately for us, she hasn't figured out why. With a sobering jerk of her head, she's back to business.

"And what are your plans for these babies after they are delivered?"

The legendary smile disappears.

"I . . . uh . . . I . . ."

Jondoe looks my way and silently pleads with to me for the answer. He wants to know for himself—for *us*, really—more than the nurse. And when I say "us" I mean all four of us: the twins, Jondoe, and me. Before I can say anything, Grace approaches my bedside.

"Both babies are in the breech position," Grace says brusquely. "Did you know that?"

I shake my head.

"Do you know what breech means?"

The image of a mare foaling hind-feet first comes to mind.

"Bottom first," I say, barely choking out the words.

"Right," Grace says. "Such deliveries pose serious health concerns for one or both of your babies." She lowers her voice, gazes at me unblinkingly. "Life-threatening concerns."

I feel woozy. I know stories of long, excruciating breech

deliveries with the most horrific outcomes. I try to steady myself with the memory of breech labors resulting in healthy bundles of joy.

She studies me in a way that makes me nervous.

"May I ask why you resisted the support of a health-care professional?" Her tone is clipped, like she's taking it personally.

"I was supposed to deliver all naturally," I reply, my voice pinched with worry.

"Well, that's not going to happen now," Grace says, tightening her smile and clapping her hands together. "You're going in for surgery."

"Surgery? I don't want to be cut open!"

Jondoe hears this and politely tries to disengage from the intake nurse without causing a stir. He smiles at her again, stunning her just long enough to sneak away.

"But you *do* want optimal care."

"Of course! But—"

"When you came through our doors, you tacitly, but legally, consented to receiving optimal care from the medical professionals at the Keystone Emergency Birthcenter as mandated by the United States government."

"I did? But—"

"No more buts." She holds up a rubber-gloved hand. "Your babies are already in a considerable amount of distress and this is the optimal care for such situations. We have a ninety-nine-percent success rate. Your surgeon is already prepping for the procedure."

"But . . . !"

Is this it? The end I have at once wished for and dreaded for so long? How could the last eight months drag so slowly, and these last few moments fly so quickly? I'm not ready!

"Relax," she says soothingly. "Let us do the thinking for you. You will be unconscious, after all."

"Why can't she be numbed from the waist down, but awake?" Jondoe asks as he flanks the opposite side of my bed. "What about an epidural or another nerve-blocker?"

I'm grateful that he knows more about my options than I do. Grace inhales sharply, glances over her shoulder, and makes eye contact with another woman in white scrubs. Then she pats me twice on my upper arm.

"We deliver hundreds of babies each week. I assure you that this is the quickest and most painless option. You'll wake up and have your babies! What could be better?"

The more she talks to me, the clearer it becomes that Grace is kind not because she's an inherently kind person. She's had to learn how to act kindly because it is the most efficient method for getting her patients in and out of the delivery room. She doesn't really care about me. She only wants good statistics to report to her superiors here at the Keystone Emergency Birthcenter.

"But what if I don't *want* quick and painless?"

Jondoe takes my hands in his. "Har—I mean, Mary, why would you ever want such a thing? You've suffered enough already just by carrying them."

Grace is gazing intently at Jondoe's face. "He makes a lot of sense. You should listen to him. I'd listen to him and I don't even know him."

"What if I want long and anguished? What if I want this experience to live with me forever?" I'm wailing now, drawing curious onlookers from far-flung corridors of the birthcenter, and I don't care. "I can't just move on with my life and never look back like this—like *they*—never existed. I refuse to forget these girls like my birthmother has forgotten me and my sister!"

The words are barely out of my mouth when the second white-scrubbed woman approaches Grace with her hands behind her back, as if she's being held captive.

"Prepartum psychosis," Grace murmurs to this anonymous healthcarer, who, without any warning, brings her hands out in the open and swiftly jabs me with a hypodermic needle in the exact spot on my arm Grace had patted moments before.

"JONDOE!"

In my pain and panic I shout out his name.

And the whole world comes to an abrupt halt.

melody
harmony

IT'S A MIRACLE I DON'T FALL RIGHT OUT OF THE BLEACHERS.

Ventura has gotten exactly the reaction she was hoping for. Though I try hard to keep myself together, I'm not doing a very convincing job of it.

"Th-that's that m-most ectopic thing you've ever said," I stammer.

"Is it? Rilly?" Her eyes are sparkling and her lips are stretched into her fullest smirk. "I know I'm right. Don't try to deny it. What I don't get is how you expect to keep this secret going."

I don't. That's what the Mission is all about.

"I mean, like, how are you gonna stop the deliveries from getting their YDNA tests? Not that the results will even be necessary because it's gonna be for seriously *obvious* that Jondoe isn't the donor when the twins come out looking nothing like him. . . ."

What?

"And bear more than a passing resemblance to the Chino-Chicano who has been so scammily posing as your platonic best friend."

Whoa. She thinks . . .

"Those twins are Zen's!"

And then Ventura folds her arms across her porny chest in triumph.

Breathe, Melody, breathe. In and out. In and out. Is this such a bad thing for Ventura to believe? It's not nearly as janked as the truth.

"First of all, I'm with Jondoe. And second of all, my bump is my business, not yours."

She laughs, but there's no joy in it.

"You have about as much chemistry with Jondoe as Harmony does with Ram."

This is so obviously true that I almost have to applaud her for being the first person to point it out.

"And it's not about business with you and Zen." Ventura pauses, smoothes her T-shirt over her flat belly, then looks up at me. "And it's not that way about Zen for me, either."

Before I can even process this information, she continues.

"You think the only reason I joined the debate team

was just so I could get you all pissy by getting into Zen's pants, right? Because that's the type of powertrippy bitch you tell everyone I am."

I wince. Those are exactly the words I've used to describe her. Such trash talk is totally against the bylaws for the Pro/Am Pregg Alliance ("respect each other's reproductive decisions"), but I can get away with such rule breaking because I'm a top-five trender on the MiNet and Ventura's popularity is limited to the Princeton Day Academy campus.

"But the truth is, I joined the debate team because I'm an awesome public speaker. Remember that speech I made right before I defeated you—by near unanimous decision—in the election of the Pro/Am President?"

How could I forget? She had singled me out as the only unhumped girl in the room, someone who couldn't possibly serve as an accurate representation of the group's commitment to our nation's reproductive prosperity. It was one of the lowest moments of my life.

"Nearly all of it was off the top of my head. I mean, like, totally made up on the spot."

If that's true, then I'm impressed. The girl definitely knows how to talk. The problem is that I am totally turned off by just about everything she talks about.

"I needed more extracurriculars so I decided to put my skills to good use by joining the debate team. Yes, Zen just happens to be the captain. But I would have joined the debate team even if it *hadn't* been Zen I'd be working so closely with every day. More to the point, I would've joined if it *had* been Zen and he was still four inches short of the minimum height requirement. I wasn't at all interested in Zen that way when I first joined."

She stops and tosses her glossy black hair over her shoulder. She's trying to come across as carefree when she is clearly feeling anything but. I should know because I'm gritting my teeth into an unnatural smile not even a sponsor could love.

"But then I got to know him," she says.

"And?" I ask, unsure of whether I want to hear the rest.

"And Zen and I have more in common than you and he do."

Her words stab me in the heart. I can't defend myself or my relationship with Zen because I'm afraid she might be right. What do we have but a history of getting on each other's nerves for sport?

"You, Melody, are living a lie. You can hate me all you want, but at least I'm honest about my ambitions. I know what I want and I'm coming to you, as one woman to another, to be up front about it."

And just when I think it can't get any worse, it does.

"You have him so no one else can have him and it's not fair," she says, standing up. "It's not fair to Zen. And, though I know you could not care less about my feelings, it's not fair to me, either."

And as she walks away, I'm left to grapple with her unspoken confession.

Ventura Vida is in love with Zen too.

harmony
melody

"WHAT HAVE YOU DONE TO HER?" JONDOE ROARS.

And all at once the whole world starts spinning again, only in the opposite direction and at ten times its normal speed.

"I KNEW IT," screams Grace, her professional façade shattered. "I'd recognize his smile anywhere!" She looks down at me in amazement. "And this is Melody Mayflower! OH MY GOD! We're delivering Melody Mayflower's twins!" She pumps her fists in the air in triumph. "Scrub up, everyone. This is our moment! We're going INTERNATIONAL! Planet Earth is about to discover the Keystone Emergency Birthcenter!"

There's a whoosh inside my head and suddenly it's like

I'm looking at the room through backwards binoculars.

I hear a chorus of voices shouting Jondoe's and Melody's names. I too need to scream, to urge Jondoe to tell the truth about us. What everyone needs to know if we're ever going to make peace with the past. It's me! Harmony Doe Smith! I'm the one about to be cut in half, not my sister!

I can't open my mouth but it hardly seems to matter. It's as if Jondoe can read my soul.

"I am who I am," Jondoe proclaims. "But that stunning girl is *not* Melody Mayflower . . ."

And at that moment another person rushes into the room with a white-coated army trailing not far behind.

"Jondoe! I got your message! I got here as fast as I could. How is Harmony . . . ?"

Ram? It sounds like Ram, but looks nothing like him. The beard is gone and he's wearing a sinfully snug T-shirt and tight trousers and I'm seeing more of his body right now than I did on our disastrous wedding night. This cannot be Ram. The injection must be taking its hallucinogenic effect.

"Harmony!" cries out Ram.

"Harmony!" cries out Jondoe.

Their voices are overpowered by uglier crashes of commotion. It would be upsetting but the noise barely reaches me now. It's all far in the distance. I'm floating above the chaos, lifted by a glorious light, rising higher and higher and higher.

I am at peace because I am not alone.

She is with me too, my birthmother, smiling beatifically, waiting to welcome me into His kingdom with open arms.

melody
harmony

I'M STILL REELING FROM THE REALIZATION THAT VENTURA
has a heart hidden underneath all that boobage.

And it's broken.

All because of me.

Gah. She really *is* as persuasive speaker. She'll make
a phenomenal politician one day because she's talked me
into the unthinkable: I feel *bad* for her. I mean, it must
not be easy for her, competing against a Hottie for Zen's
attention and affection. My presence at PDA is pretty
inescapable. My image is all over this school, from the
PregGo Bars in the vending machines to the National
Association for Procreation posters on the walls. If *I'm*
sick of seeing my face everywhere, I can't even imagine
how she must feel about it. It's no wonder she negs so

hard on me. It all makes sense now.

The door to the gym bangs open and I'm not thinking much about Ventura Vida's feelings anymore. Zen races through the entrance faster than I've ever seen him run.

Ventura must have threatened to go public with her accusations. And Zen is wanking out about it because he doesn't know any better not to. Zen's got an overloaded brain cache, but he isn't adequately versed in the ways of female scheming because he can't get this kind of knowledge on the quikiwiki. No, it's embedded in our XX chromosomes, like hemophilia and red-green colorblindness.

I know Ventura would *never* go to the MiNet with her gossip, not if she holds any hope of actually winning him away from me. Ventura is savvy enough to understand that betraying him—betraying *both* of us—would only bring Zen and me closer together, which is the last thing she wants right now. What *does* she hope to achieve by blackmailing us? That's harder to figure out. I can't underestimate Ventura's ruthless intelligence. I'm positive that she's already anticipating my response and plotting her counter-move. All this girl-on-girl hate is *exhausting*. Sometimes I wish we could dose on testosterone, punch each other in the face, and get it over with already.

Zen is running around in circles, swiveling his head all around, trying to find me among all the preggers sitting in the bleachers. I leap—well, I'm incapable of leaping—I lurch to my feet.

"Zen!"

It would be a very romantic moment if I wasn't saddled with forty excess pounds of synthetic and possibly parasitic skinfeel. I wave my arms to get his attention, which is totally unnecessary because I'm not easy to miss. Zen cuts straight through the Quidditch match in progress and almost gets taken down by a Beater hurling a Nerf quaffle right at his machopartes, but he's saved by the same lightning-quick reflexes that serve him so well in Ping-Pong.

By the time he gets to me, he's practically staggering and can't catch his breath.

"Jondoe [pant] . . . MiNet . . . [pant] . . ."

I help him out by doing the talking for him.

"I know! She told me! Ventura thinks you're the donor!"

He's slicing his hands through the air, shaking his head *nononononono*.

"The [pant] . . . truth [pant] . . ."

Zen really needs to do more cardio. He looks like he's about to puke, but that's not stopping him from yanking on my arm to make me follow him back down the bleachers.

"Ow!" I say, trying to shake him off. "Dose down, Zen. She doesn't know the truth. No one knows the truth."

"You're not getting it!" he gasps. "The whole world knows now!"

And he shoves his MiVu Mini right under my nose with one hand while trying to drag me out of the gym with the other. "Now."

I'm about to ask Zen how he hacked the campus

MiNet blind *again* when seeing and hearing Jondoe takes *my* breath away.

"*Harmony is in the operating room right now, making our deliveries. That's right. Our deliveries. I'm here to make things right. I'm the father of Harmony's twins, not Ram. I did not bump with Melody Mayflower. Not because I couldn't—I'm as potent as ever and totally could have bumped it out on the first try if I wanted to—but I didn't even try. After I met her sister, Harmony, I was thinking more with my heart than my . . .*"

It's just like Zen said. Jondoe. On the MiNet. Telling the world the truth.

BORN AGAIN

Faith is confidence in what we hope for and assurance about what we do not see.

—Hebrews 11:1

melody

WE HAD NO TIME TO WASTE. WITHIN A MINUTE OF SEEING JON-doe on the MiVu, I dashed out of the gym, across the campus, through the parking lot, and into the passenger side of Zen's car. I didn't think I was still capable of run-ning at all, let alone sprinting, but it's amazing what a terrified rush of adrenaline can do.

Zen and I didn't speak until we had put at least a half mile between us and the school. This took literally, like, ten seconds. Only then did I realize that we weren't in Zen's VW Plug at all.

"Zen! Whose car is this? Gah!"

"Asif's," Zen said, checking the rearview.

"Zen! Aren't we in enough trouble already?"

"The paparazzi know my car, Mel. They're gonna be

looking for it," he says as he programs the autodrive. "We had to *borrow* Asif's Aero if we had any chance of getting away before the media surrounded the school."

"But did you have to steal a quarter-million-dollar sports car?"

"It's hardly grand theft auto when the owner doesn't bother to password-protect his keycode. And Asif will thank us for *borrowing* his car because he's dying to get in the famegame, and this model Aero will ultimately become identified as a notorious part of our getaway and he'll start trending just by association." Zen's eyes are wandering all around. He's obviously MiNetting right in front of me. "And we needed something fast if we want to get to the birth center before . . ." His voice trails off. "Oh." Then again. "Oh!"

"What is it? Did something happen to Harmony?"

The thought of Harmony in the stirrups brings tears to my eyes, which mucks up my MiNet. I wink-right-left-right-blink-blink-double-wink but I can't log on.

"She delivered the twins!" Zen cheers.

"She did? When? I knew she wasn't telling me the truth last night! Arrrrgh! I can't get on!" I try to rub the moisture out of my eyes. "Why is my MiNet so janked right now? Tell me what's happening!"

"There's nothing to see! She's not on camera. She's still recovering. According to medical professionals at the Keystone Emergency Birthcenter, twin girls were delivered via C-section. . . ."

I tell myself that this is normal. I personally know dozens of girls who have been sliced open, not to mention millions of anonymous girls all around the world. But this is different. This is my *sister* being cut in half.

"The twins were breech and this was the optimal choice for delivery."

I can't even hear what he's saying now because my ears are ringing with the roar of my stifled tears.

"Mel, what's wrong? Harmony's fine. . . ."

And that's when I start bawling.

"They just cut her open!" I yell. "How is that fine?"

"It was the optimal choice for delivery. . . ." he repeats.

I wipe my eyes with my sleeve, desperate to see for myself what's happening to my sister.

"This is all my fault."

"How is this possibly your fault?"

"THIS. IS. ALL. MY. FAULT."

I'm inconsolable because it's true.

"*You* didn't get her pregnant. She got herself pregnant when she decided to have sex with Jondoe. It was her choice. Not yours."

"I should have never let her come here. I should have sent her back to Goodside when I had the chance."

"She came here to escape her oppressive life in Goodside, Mel. She didn't want to be married to Ram. She came here . . ." His eyes are darting back and forth faster than I ever thought possible. "Oh! Sweet Darwin!"

"What! What?"

"Your parents are doing a Q&A . . ."

"My parents know that I'm not pregging?"

"Why don't you understand this? *Everyone* on the MiNet knows."

I'm bruising my eyeballs, I'm winking and blinking so hard.

"Why can't I log on?"

"Yeah. About that." He smiles sheepishly. "I took the liberty of preemptively taking you off the grid."

"You! The anti-censorship crusader! Who has never NOT hacked into a MiNet blind! You! Have taken *me!* Off the grid! Gahhhh!"

Yelling nonsensically isn't working, so I reel back and punch him as hard as I can in his Ping-Pong serving arm.

"Owwwww! I did it for your own good!"

"Put me back on right now! I need to know what's going on!"

"Trust me, Mel, you don't need to know any more about what's happening than what I'm telling you. You don't want to see what the haters are saying about you right now."

I can only imagine what the MiNet reaction is to Jondoe's confession. I'm counterfeit. A renegger. A janky famegamer who didn't deserve to get breedy with the likes of a perfect specimen like Jondoe in the first place. But I really don't care about a plunge in my popularity rankings right now. In truth, I'd welcome it.

"YOU'RE NOT TELLING ME ANYTHING. TELL ME WHAT MY PARENTS ARE SAYING RIGHT NOW."

Zen sticks his finger in his ear and adjusts his earbud.

"I can't hear anything if you keep screaming into my ear."

I clamp my mouth shut and watch Zen as he watches my parents on the MiNet. He's trying to keep a straight face, but his mouth is all twitchy. After a few seconds of silence his jaw goes slack. "Oooooooooh."

"What?"

"Yeah . . . um . . . Your parents are . . ."

"WHAT?"

Disowning me. Unadopting me. Arranging a return on damaged merchandise with Good Shepherd Family Placement Services.

"Defending you."

"What?" I hit him again. "What do you mean? What are they saying *specifically*?"

"Well," his eyes flit back and forth. "They're saying that no way could any daughter of theirs have done something like this because they didn't raise you that way."

They didn't raise me at all. They outsourced to a team of experts.

He tilts his head as if to get a better listen. "You are

a young woman of honor and integrity, who has never disappointed them or anyone you've ever made a promise to."

I'm stunned. I've never heard my parents say anything like this about me before. Honor and integrity are not quantifiable high-revenue qualities that promise a solid return on the parental unit's investment.

This doesn't sound like Ash and Ty. At all.

"I don't believe you."

"I'm just reporting what they're saying . . ."

"Which you wouldn't even have to do if you weren't such a MiNet-blinding hackass . . ."

He shushes me. "Ash and Ty are saying that you have always taken your reproductive responsibilities very seriously and . . ." He looks at me. "You sure you want to hear this?"

I nod.

"They're accusing Jondoe of pulling this stunt to grab attention for his flaccid brand; you know, because he hasn't officially bumped anyone since The Hotties went public. They're saying you have too much compassion for the Jaydens to participate in such a scummy scam."

Compassion. Another low-value trait I was never encouraged to develop. Do my parents really believe what they're saying? Or are they following a PR script?

"Have Lib or the Jaydens gone public yet?"

Zen shakes his head. "No, they're conspicuously absent

from the media frenzy. They're probably headed to the birthcenter right now, just like us."

He pauses, then looks at me in a way that lets me know that I've got his full attention. At least for the moment.

"Do you know what you're going to say when we get to the birthcenter? By the time we get there, the place will be surrounded."

"I have no idea what I'm going to say to the Jaydens," I reply, my mind spinning with inadequate apologies. "What can I possibly say?"

"Um." Zen sucks on his teeth. "I meant your official statement to the media. The one we've been working on. Because the time is now."

I glare at him with equal measures of disgust and disbelief.

"I know this isn't how we thought it would happen—Jondoe kind of stole our moment—but that doesn't mean that you can't take it back from him. All eyes will be on you, Mel, and when you reveal that fake belly, you are representing all the girls who have been victims of preggsploitation!"

It's almost impossible to make Zen listen when he's going manifesto, but I try anyway.

"The Mission is not topping my to-do list. My first priority is making sure Harmony is safe. My second priority is making things right with the Jaydens. . . ."

Zen isn't hearing a word I'm saying.

"And when you make a pro-prophylactic statement about the freedom to have sex without getting pregnant, the whole world will be listening—"

"I don't want to be a pro-prophylactic icon!" I shout over him. "I never did!"

This shuts him up. "What are you talking about?

"I'm not against condoms as, like, a concept. I think they *should* be made available to teens who want them."

"So what's the problem? Say *that!*"

I shake my head. "I'm not comfortable with the idea of telling other girls how to run their sex lives. I never was."

"You earned seven figures in endorsement deals telling other girls exactly how to run their sex lives!"

"I know! I'm a hypocrite!" I bury my face in my hands. "And I deserve to rot in Harmony's version of Hell."

"But we used to brainstorm solutions for the Virus all the time."

"That was just talk to pass the downtime."

But I always knew it was so much more than "just talk" to Zen. The whole time he was laying the groundwork for something bigger. Much bigger. He had a vision for a group of reproductive freedom fighters called Contra/Ception, who would change history by pulling pranks, not triggers. Like, we would distribute candy birth-control pills on Halloween. Or hack all the digital billboards in New York City, London, Tokyo, Mumbai, and Beijing to display slogans like TO BREED OR NOT TO

My mission? Zen wants me to hold a press conference right after Harmony delivers. I'll lift my shirt to reveal Zen's Contra/Ception logo tattooed across the B$B. I'll apply the serum and make an impassioned speech about passing pro-prophylactic legislation as my fake pregg melts away in front of billions of MiNet viewers. . . .

I was never quite as convinced as he was.

"Then why did you agree to support the Mission if you didn't want to?" he asks.

There's no point in holding back anymore.

"For *you*, you big jerk. Because the Mission was important to you. And I wanted to be important to you too."

His face softens. "But . . . Mel . . . You already . . ." His face startles. "Whoa."

"What?"

"It's Ram. Wow. He cut off his beard. And he's with some other Goodsider dude with a huge Adam's Apple."

"Zeke?"

"Who's Zeke? Anyway . . . Ram's . . . ohhhh . . . whoooooa."

That's it. I'm taking matters into my own hands. I lunge for the MiVuMini I hope is in his pocket. "Gimme it! I want it! Now!"

"As much as I've always wanted you to so aggressively try to get into my pants," Zen says, laughing nervously, "I'm afraid I can't let you have the goods."

"I'm not taking no for an answer!" I put all my extra weight into wrestling the MiVuMini out of Zen's jeans. I plunge my hand into his pocket and pull it out triumphantly.

"I feel so violated," Zen says, half joking.

"I so don't care. Not even ish," I say, searching for Ram's feed. When I find it, I can't quite believe my eyes. "He cut off his beard! And he's dressed like a normal person!"

I've never seen Ram in anything other than his Goodside suit. This slim T-shirt and snug jeans leave far less to the imagination. I hate to say it, but Ram is actually kinda hot. Unfortunately for Zeke, his Otherside makeover isn't quite as effective. Just as Ram opens his mouth to speak, Zeke boldly and unapologetically takes his hand.

"Did he . . . ?" Zen asks, eyes flashing.

"He did!"

"Is he . . . ?"

I'm afraid to say what I know both of us are thinking.

"Shhh. Just listen."

"Jondoe is telling the truth. The twins are his, not mine," Ram is saying. "But ya'll must understand that Harmony is not an adulteress. She did not cheat on me because we were never married in the eyes of God."

"Remember when he said that last spring?" Zen asks.

I shush him again because I have a feeling that I'm about to find out if my instincts are right.

"I am a gay American!" he cries out exultantly, holding up his and Zeke's interlocked hands. "We are gay Americans for God!"

"Well," Zen says, nonplussed. "That's the only part of this whole mess that actually makes sense."

harmony
melody

I AWAKE TO WOMBLIKE WARMTH AND DARKNESS. SOMEONE IS humming a song I've never heard before.

"Mother?" I whisper. "Is that you?"

Suddenly Jondoe's face is before me. "Harmony! You're awake."

He speaks so softly I can barely hear him over the humming, which, as I listen harder, isn't one voice but many voices. And somewhere in the distance.

"Where is she? My mother?"

She looked just like me and Melody, just older. I saw wisdom in her eyes, compassion in her kind smile. She had answers. She could tell me what to do.

"Your mother?" he asks. "She's still in Goodside." He glances toward the heavily curtained windows, where the humming is coming from. "Look, Harmony, we might have only a few minutes together—"

"My *birth*mother," I say more forcefully. "I saw my birthmother. I *saw* her . . ."

Jondoe eyes me warily.

"Saw her *where*, Harmony? I promise you that security isn't letting anyone in here who doesn't need to be."

"But I *saw* her! In the clouds! She was welcoming me to Heaven!"

When Jondoe shushes me I realize how . . . how *god-freakish* I must sound right now.

"Heaven has to make do with one less angel for at least another day. Because you're still here. On earth. With me."

I know he's right. And yet, the Heavenly picture of my mother in my head is more vivid than Jondoe standing right beside me. He flashes a smile meant to reassure me that everything is right between us. But it's a strained smile, which makes me even more nervous than if he hadn't smiled at all.

"You're still under the influence of Obliterall, that's all."

Obliterall. Yes. That would explain why I'm still numbed, inside and out.

Jondoe casts another look toward the curtains.

"This is a lot to take in right now, especially when you're still dosed, but you need to know that the press is practically rioting outside the hospital. They're really putting my security detail to the test. The National Guard might have to be called in."

"What?"

"Legally, the birthcenter has to wait until you've completed the minimum post-partum recovery period before they can let anyone see you. The media has already got you on the clock. You'll get another forty-six minutes and eighteen seconds and not a moment more before you have to make some sort of statement, though I'm pretty sure I can charm Grace into taking extra measures to protect our privacy. . . ."

I'm listening to what he's saying but none of it is making much sense.

"But . . . why . . . ?"

"I told the truth, Harmony."

It's Ram. With Zeke Yoder following behind. And before he says it, I know the truth he's referring to. I've known it all along.

"I'm a gay American, Harmony," Ram says proudly. "I'm a gay American for God."

"That's what he told the MiNet," Jondoe says with a slightly disbelieving tone. "So the whole world would know that you hadn't cheated on him because you were never truly bound together by marriage in, you know, a carnal way."

"You did?" I ask.

"I did!" Ram boasts. Then his face falls and he guiltily scuffs a pointy-toed shoe across the floor. "I guess I shoulda told you first, then the whole world."

"There wasn't much time Ram," Jondoe asserts. "There still isn't much time. . . ."

"Besides, there wasn't anything to tell," I say. "I always knew about you, Ram. The whole settlement knew, especially after you were caught looking at those pictures. . . ."

"What pictures?" Jondoe asks.

Ram blushes and shifts uneasily. "Just pictures, okay?" he says defensively.

Even now, years later, and after his world declaration, Ram is still shamed by the private stash of vintage pornographic magazines he'd hidden—not well enough—in the hayloft.

"We've always been the different ones," I say. "The ones who couldn't conform to the Orders, no matter how hard we prayed. That's why they put us together." I turn to smile at Zeke. Thank goodness he came to this conclusion *before* he married and fathered a child. "I'm happy that you've found someone who makes you happy."

I reach out my hand for Ram to hold and am touched when he actually takes it. Oddly enough, the three of us-Ram, Zeke, and me—holding hands like this is no doubt the most tender moment of our marriage.

"And I always knew about you and him," he says, glancing at Jondoe. "But I was afraid to confront you because I didn't know what the Elders would do to me if you left me. . . ."

"Well, from the looks of you two," Jondoe says wryly, "it seems like you've embraced life on this side of the Gates."

Ram and Zeke exchange bashful smiles.

"I reckon we have," Ram says. "And I wouldn't have had the courage to be me if it hadn't been for you."

"What did I do?" I ask.

"You were brave enough to break the Orders," he says, "and not look back."

Brave? *Me?* If only he knew how petrified I've felt this entire time.

Ram lets go of my hand and steps away from the bed.

"You two have a lot of fat to chew," Ram says.

"We'll stand guard outside the door," Zeke adds. "Keep the trespassers out."

"Thank you," Jondoe and I say at the same time as the couple exits the room.

Jondoe fixes his eyes on mine, doesn't blink.

"I also told the truth, Harmony. About everything."

Only then do I place a hand on my emptied belly and remember.

The twins.

Oh my grace.

The twins.

melody
harmony

THE WHOLE WORLD KNOWS THAT I'M THE MOST INFAMOUSLY mocked-up pregger in history. This is major gossip. A number-one trender for sure. So it's a bit surprising to me when Zen is able to drive all the way to the Keystone Emergency Birthcenter without any slow-downs. I figured that all the roads leading up to the birthcenter would be traffic-jammed by professional scummers and amateur gossipmongers.

"Hmmm . . ." Zen says, double-checking the MapApp. "Did the media get lost?"

"Maybe I'm not nearly as popular as I thought I was," I say hopefully. "Maybe this story isn't that major after all."

"They could be covering Ram's coming out," Zen suggests, though I can tell that he isn't quite convinced.

And for about two seconds, I'm allowed to believe that I'll be left alone. Then Zen turns into the driveway leading to the Birthcenter, and our peace is pierced by the peal and squeal of tires.

"What's happening?"

No less than a dozen on- and off-road vehicles have come roaring out of the woods and are now overtaking us from all sides.

"Doooooo sooooomethiiiiiing!"

"I caaaaaaaan't!"

The autodrive brings the car to a screeching halt.

So *that's* why the route was clear. The way through had been cleared for us, to guarantee that we would drive right into their trap. By the time we realize our mistake, it's already too late. The Aero is surrounded: dead-ended at the front and trapped from behind.

"Harmony and Ram would have seen this coming," I say.

"How?" Zen says, eyes ablaze.

"It was just like herding cattle for the slaughter."

harmony
melody

"HAVE YOU SEEN THEM YET?" I WHISPER.

"No," Jondoe replies softly.

"Do you want to see them?"

"I'm scared."

"Me too."

But I know I must.

I can't make this decision without seeing them first.

melody
harmony

A DOZEN OF THE HUGEST MEN I'VE EVER LAID EYES ON ARE closing in on the Aero. All are in black and masked, so you can't blame me for letting out a scream when one of them gently—even politely—taps on the glass to get my attention.

"I *told* you the U.S. government has been experimenting with half-human, half-cyborg hybrids!"

Zen seriously can't stop with the conspiracy theories, even in a crisis.

The largest one taps again. "You need to come with us."

"I think I recognize them! I think they're part of Jondoe's security team!"

"Are you sure? How do you know? I'm not going with them!"

"One of these guys could pick up this car and crumple it under his armpit if he wanted to."

"That's not making me feel any better about opening this door."

"There's no point in hiding if they're going to get to us anyway. And I really think they're with Jondoe. Besides, what other option do we have?"

And for what might be the first time in history, Zen has nothing.

We open the door and immediately one of the body-guards lifts me up and carries me through the crowd that has quickly assembled from its hiding spot on the other side of the building. I scream, but I can't even hear myself over the roar. I'm blinded by the paparazzi glare and can't see what is happening to Zen—or myself, for that matter.

I'm put down onto a hard surface. By the time my eyes readjust, I realize I'm in the back of one of the off-roaders that cut us off and one of the bodyguards is in there with me.

"Wait! The birthcenter is that way! Where are you taking me?"

The bodyguard takes off his mask, and what's under-neath is even more intimidating. Every bone in this man's face looks like it's been broken at least twice and crudely put back together as some sort of cubist sculp-tural experiment.

"To the nearest juvenile detention center," he says, flashing a police badge. "You're under arrest."

My self-defense reflexes don't stand a chance against a bruiser like this.

Yes. That's what I'm thinking as he pulls my arms around my back and clamps down the handcuffs. That all the Krav Maga training my parents paid for—like everything else, apparently—was a total waste of my time and their resources.

harmony
melody

GRACE PUSHES A WHEELCHAIR INTO THE ROOM, ALL SMILES. It's a birthday of sorts for her too. She'll never have to toil away in anonymity ever again. She'll build a whole second career out of being the caregiver who delivered the most famous twins in the world. This is the greatest day of her life.

"Harmony wants to see them," Jondoe says, before adding, "*I* want to see them."

"We've already cleared this floor for your privacy."

Grace has a hard time taking her eyes off him. He's got a magnetic quality that makes him unlookawayable. But that's not really him, that's just his image. I'd like to think that the Jondoe I've seen—the one who cut my hair, the one who coached me through my labor pains this morning, the one who took control of the transport, the one who keeps squeezing my shoulders reassuringly, the one who is all the more interesting for his imperfect unpredictability—is the real him.

I hope that he's gotten a chance to see me for who I am too.

Grace swoons as Jondoe effortlessly scoops me out of the bed and sets me down in the wheelchair. She does her best to resume a businesslike air as we make our way down the hall, where two burly guards are standing on opposite sides of a long pane of glass.

"They're in there," Grace says, gesturing toward the window, which is low enough for me to look in without getting out of the wheelchair.

And there they are.

Two pink, pinch-faced slumbering bundles.

The twins.

I don't cry. I thought I would cry. With joy, with sorrow. But I don't cry. I just . . .

Look.

One bundle yawns. The other crinkles her tiny nose.

My chest starts to ache. At first I think it's because my milk is coming in. But then I realize that it's because I've been holding my breath this entire time.

"You can go in, if you like," Grace says encouragingly, mostly to Jondoe. I think she's dying for the opportunity to see him holding a gorgeous baby in the crook of each muscled arm.

"Do I have to nurse them? Because my milk hasn't come in yet. . . ."

Grace laughs and pats my head condescendingly. "*Nurse* them? Oh, you won't be able to do that until tomorrow at the earliest."

"What? Why?"

"Only the tiniest fraction of our patients choose that method of nutritional delivery. It's standard operating procedure to give all patients a dose of Stoplac, the lactation suppression medication—"

I interrupt her. "So I *don't* have to nurse them?"

"Oh no," she says. "Our nutritive formula is even *better* than breast milk, I promise you. I thought you might want to go in and *hold* them since, well, they are yours to keep. . . ."

Mine to keep.

I shake my head silently.

"Are you sure?" Jondoe asks.

His voice rouses me. I'd actually forgotten that I wasn't alone in this. That he too was seeing his daughters for the first time.

"Harmony?" he says, talking to me but gaping at the babies through the window.

"Please take me back to my room," I say. "I've seen enough."

melody
harmony

I'M NOT IN LOCKDOWN. YET.

No, I'm in the place where underage rule breakers like me are detained until we can meet with our parents and get all lawyered up to face whatever criminal charges are being leveled against us. The Picasso-faced policeman read me my rights and informed me that the Jaydens have already come after me with two counts of "commercial procreative malfeasance." I knew they would, but I guess I didn't think it would happen so quickly. I thought I'd have time to see Harmony at the hospital.

Not knowing anything about her current condition is the hardest part about being stuck in here right now. That, and having no idea what's happened to Zen since I last saw him in the parking lot. Technically, he didn't break any laws. But maybe they've got him locked up here too? As a co-conspirator? No one is telling me anything.

It's an airless cinderblock room furnished with a conference table and half a dozen chairs. That's it. I think I'm supposed to sit here and reflect on my crimes. The Jaydens are just the beginning of my legal troubles. It's pretty much a given that every corporation that has ever hired The Hotties will sue us for "negligent misrepresentation" of our brand. I'm feeling claustrophobic, but it doesn't have anything to do with the stale, antiseptic atmosphere. This B$B is crushing me, like, *literally*. All I can focus on right now is how badly I want to get it taken off. I've tried to relay a message to my parents about where I've stashed the removal serum, but I have no idea if they received it, or would be inclined to do me the favor of retrieving it even if they had.

Now that everyone knows the truth about me—that I'm shadiest counterfeiter since Surrogetting was legalized—there's no point in dragging the belly around anymore. Well, I suppose a judge could think of a valid reason to keep it. I don't know what the minimum lockdown guidelines are for my crimes, but there could be no crueler—or fitting—punishment than being forced to wear this mutating skinfeel monstrosity for the duration of my sentence.

No one—not the police, not the administrative assistants, not the guards at the door—look at me all starstruck anymore. No one asks for my autograph or rubs my belly for luck. Everyone regards me with disgust, and these are people who deal with sketchy, down-market types all day long. To these patriotic public servants, I've committed what amounts to reproductive treason. I haven't just hurt the Jaydens, my parents, or my own future. I've hurt *America*.

I hear voices outside in the hall. I know I should be busting a clot right now. But I'm oddly at peace with the idea of facing my parents. The lies are over. And I have nothing else to hide.

The door opens and Ash and Ty step into the room. It's actually kind of weird to see them all 4-D in my facespace and not flat on screen. Without the benefit of professional hair and makeup, or the real-time appearance autocorrect app, they look less like the glamorous Surrogetting gurus that they are, and more like the ordinary—if hyper intensely strategic—middle-aged mom and dad they used to be. They're alone, which is unexpected. I thought for sure they'd have their attorneys in tow.

I stand up and brace myself on the conference table for the monumental ass-spanking I know I deserve.

But Ash and Ty give me the shock of my life—a life that has been marked by anonymous birthparents, secret twinhood, and fake preggings—by not saying anything at all, rushing over to my side of the tiny room, lifting up my MyTurnTee, and pressing their cold hands all over my infamous ginormity.

"Hands off!" I recoil from their touch and defensively

pull my shirt back down.

"We knew it!" Ash cries out.

"Knew *what*?"

"That Jondoe is lying!" Ty replies. "That you really are pregging with his babies!"

Gah. This is going to be way harder than I thought.

"No, I'm not. He's telling the truth," I say quickly because I've got more pressing concerns. "How is Harmony? Where is Zen?"

My parents exchange knowing looks. My mother mouths, *prepartum psychosis*. . . .

"I *saw* that! I am not suffering from prepartum psychosis because I'm *not* pregging! Now tell me what's going on with Harmony and Zen!"

My mother takes me by the hand and tries to get me to sit down, but I resist.

"Tell me!"

Ash lets out an annoyed groan. Any time she gives in to my demands, she feels like she's contributing to our nation's downward spiral by failing to live up to China's totalitarian parental standards.

"Well, Harmony did major damage to your brand," she begins. "She chopped off all her hair and dyed what was left of it black. *Black!* She doesn't look anything like you anymore."

"What? When I saw her she'd only cut off the braid. She dyed it black?"

I'm having trouble picturing what Harmony would

look like . . . if she doesn't look like me anymore.

"This renders our synergistic six-month re-branding initiative totally obsolete, of course," Ty says. "All that strategizing, gone to waste."

"Maybe the timing isn't so bad after all," Ash replies. "We always knew Melody would have to make over her image after the deliveries were made, to launch herself as an independent entity, separate from her other half—"

"Listen to you two! My twin sister just had an emergency C-section and my best friend is probably being waterboarded right now for all I know, and all you two can talk about is *hair* and *branding*?"

What makes people so morally bankrupt? I never met my grandparents—they all took a dirt nap before I came around—so I have no idea if they raised Ash and Ty to be so famegamey and moneygrubby. Right now I'm going with Darwin: DNA is destiny. Otherwise I'm humped.

"You need to calm yourself down right now," Ash says. "All that stress cannot be good for the twins. I'm surprised your MOM alarm isn't going off right now. . . ."

And that's when *I* go off.

"FOR THE LAST MUTHERHUMPING TIME, I'M NOT PREGGING," I shout loud enough to penetrate the soundproof walls. "I can prove it right now! Did you get that bottle I asked for back at the house?"

"We did," my father says, "but we turned it over to the authorities."

"What?"

My mother assumes her concerned face. "We understand that a girl at your level in the famegame moves with a fast crowd. It's one of the risks. You get exposed to too much too soon. If you have experimented with a new controlled substance, we would be remiss as parents if we didn't alert—"

"It's not a drug!" I protest. "It's the removal serum for the Billion Dollar Belly! It's ALTERR. Artificial Living Technology . . . no . . . Tissue! Artificial Living *Tissue* . . . um . . ." I struggle to remember the rest of the acronym. "Whatever! It doesn't matter what it's called. It's the next-generation FunBump. . . ."

The more I talk, the more skeptical my parents look. And I don't blame them because I sound for seriously psycho right now.

"I know it sounds crazy, but I'm telling you the truth. I'm mocked up!"

Ty nods at Ash, who closes her eyes in resignation.

"Okay," Ash says.

"Okay . . . what?"

Ash and Ty nod at each other again, like a secret signal for something to begin.

"We have always expected you to perform to the highest standards," Ash says, "but we never asked you to do anything you weren't capable of achieving. You have always proven us right by not just achieving, but *excelling* academically, athletically, artistically. You have never failed at any task we've set forth before you."

231

"Until now," Ty adds.

"Right," Ash says with a slight wince. "Until now. But would you have pushed yourself as hard as we pushed you?"

"No way," Ty answers.

They're right about that.

"The one downside to all your success is that you aren't equipped to deal with failure," Ty says. "So when you put yourself in a negative outcome situation, you felt compelled to cover it up rather than disappoint us."

Ash and Ty clasp hands, then reach out for mine to join them in what I know from their BestEgg seminars is called the Ring of Truth. I stuff my hands into my pockets, which is very immature but whatever. I'm over this whole conversation because it's clear to me that I won't get any information out of them about Harmony or Zen.

"But we're ready to accept the shameful truth, Melody," Ash says. "We won't love you any less."

She's looking at me expectantly, like she's still waiting for me to make a confession.

"I've already *told* you. I'm not pregging!"

Ash inhales sharply. She's losing her patience. "Your secret is out, Melody. Your friend has been telling everyone the truth."

"What secret? What friend? Shoko?" There's no way she would ever sell me out. And besides, she still thinks I'm carrying Jondoe's twins. I don't believe it.

"No, not *her*," my mother says dismissively. "The more

232

up-market one. The gorgeous Eurasian girl . . ."

Ventura Vida. That powertrippy bitch.

"What's *she* saying?"

Ash unleashes an exasperated sigh. "Why do you insist on dragging this out? She's telling everyone the truth! That the twins aren't Jondoe's, they're Zen's!"

"Whaaaaaaaaaaaaaaaat?"

I guess Ventura has given up. And if she can't hump Zen, she'll humiliate me.

Ty shakes his head disappointedly. "I knew your unusually close friendship with him was a problem. No guy wants to keep it platonic! Ever!"

"We understand why you wanted to hide the truth," Ash is saying. "But this may not be such a disaster. Zen has grown up a lot in the past year. He's smart and *does* meet the minimum height requirement. It's possible that the Jaydens may still go ahead with the deal. And if they don't, I'm sure that there will be another couple who would be more than happy to—"

"WHY WON'T YOU EVER LISTEN TO ME?" I scream. "I'M NOT PREGGING WITH ZEN OR JON-DOE OR ANYONE!"

And that's when I decide to put an end to the lies once and for all, in the most dramatic and indisputable way I can think of.

I climb up onto the conference table . . .

My parents are screaming for security.

Take a deep breath . . .

The door flies open and a bodyguard rushes in.
Close my eyes . . .
More screaming.
And take a flying leap.

harmony
melody

WE'RE BACK AT THE ROOM NOW, UNDER THE PRETENSE THAT I need my rest.

"You'll be pleased to know that the Newborn Quality Testing Service has scored both girls in the highest percentile for preemies born five weeks early," Grace gushes with a sort of pride that would be deemed sinful even if she had been the one who birthed the babies. "They might have to stay in the hospital for a short while to get their weight up, but otherwise they're thriving."

I heave a sigh of relief. At least they have that going for them. They aren't starting their lives off at a sickly disadvantage, like Melody and me.

"They're small, but strong," Jondoe says, running his finger along my cheek. "Like you."

"Oh," Grace says coquettishly. "You're not giving yourself enough credit for your half of the DNA. You *are* the all-time highest scorer on the Standards, after all. Thanks to you and the *hundreds* of deliveries to which you donated your genetic material, America just might have a shot at reclaiming its top spot in the world rankings."

I don't understand most of what she's saying, but Jondoe does. A strange look passes over Jondoe's face, one I've never seen before. It's a wary awakening of sorts, a dawning of knowledge that he isn't quite ready to process.

"Can you please excuse us?" I ask, interrupting Grace.

"Of course," she says, looking wounded. "I should check up on security anyway. We have a . . . a . . . *situation* brewing on another floor. . . ."

I wait until she's in the hall before asking, "Are you okay?"

He backs himself into the wheelchair, bends forward at the waist, and presses his face into his hands. I've never seen him in such a state of quiet despair.

"What's wrong?"

"The babies," he says.

"What about the babies?"

He looks up at me miserably.

"I never thought about them," he says, "as people."

I ease myself out of the bed to console him. I wobble when my feet first touch the floor and have to brace myself on the bed as I inch my way to the wheelchair that Grace brought for me, not him. I'm surprised not to feel much discomfort at all, considering I was cut open just a few hours ago. My belly is more sore than painful, remarkably similar to how I feel if I've spent hours bending and twisting at the waist to pick wild strawberries. I suppose this makes sense. The less pain I feel, the more willing I'll be to get pregnant again. As if that's all there is to it.

"Jondoe," I say. "What's this about?"

He looks up to see that I'm out of bed and immediately springs out of the wheelchair. "You shouldn't be on your feet right now! You need to recover!"

"I'm fine . . ."

He's not hearing it. He insists on pulling me into the wheelchair. If he's being overprotective, it's only because he cares. And he cares not because I'm a potential vessel for future offspring, but because I'm *me*.

He hops up on the edge of the hospital bed.

"The babies," he repeats.

I nod to encourage him to continue.

"They're all, like, a part of me," he says, "And I'm a part of them. Only I'm not. Because they're all out there living their lives and I have nothing to do with them. Like, any bundle in a stroller could be mine, only the baby isn't mine. He or she was bought by someone else. That baby could grow up to be president someday. Or that baby could grow up to be a serial killer. . . ."

"Don't say that!"

"It's *true*, Harmony! These babies can grow up to do or be anything—good, bad, or boring—but none of them would be here if it weren't for me. That's, like, a lot of responsibility, only without *any* of the responsibility!"

"You never thought about this before?"

"I was encouraged to think about everything *but* that," he says.

"And you're not allowed to have contact with any of those babies to see how they turned out?"

He shakes his head. "No. My agency tracks all deliveries with my DNA, keeping an eye on Future Up-and-Comers. But I've never actually seen any of them."

"You mean after they've been placed with their new parents?"

"I mean *ever*," he says. "And up until now, I was like"—he pantomimes wiping his brow—"*Whew! What a relief. Who needs that hassle?* But I don't know . . ." He scratches his light beard, the real one, each hair a fine golden thread.

"What are you saying?" I ask. "That you want to be . . . a father?"

He pauses midscratch.

"I've already been a father many times over," Jondoe says. "But until I met you, I've never gave a single thought about being a *dad*."

melody
harmony

MY HEAD IS THROBBING, HEAVY.

"Where am I?"

"You're at the Emergency Birthcenter."

It's my mother's voice, but I can't quite focus on the visuals just yet.

When she comes fully into view, I see her pressing her head into my father's shoulder. Both Ash and Ty sniffling and blinking away tears. I have never seen either of them cry before. Am I hallucinating? I rub my throbbing temple. I feel like I'm wearing a concussion ice pack, but I'm not. I can't remember what happened. Did I miscalculate my aerodynamic trajectory and whack my head on the floor? I thought for sure my belly would have cushioned my fall. . . .

My belly.

I grab my skinny midsection.

My Billion Dollar Belly is gone!

I lift up my shirt and rub my hands all over my pale, stretch-mark-free tummy. It's a little softer than it was before the scam, but I guess that's to be expected when I haven't done so much as a single crunch in eight and a half months. The strange thing is, even though I *see* that the B$B is gone, I can still feel every ounce of those extra forty pounds. I don't feel any lighter now than I did before its removal.

"How?" I'm overwhelmed by questions. "When?"

"We brought you back here because we thought you would misdeliver after you . . ." Ash pinches her lips together, inhales. "After you did what you did."

"We thought you had gone crazy and had tried to t—" Not even Ty can say the word; he has to spell it out. "T-E-R-M-I-N-A-T-E."

They tell me one of the bodyguards broke my fall and immediately injected me with a heavy-duty sedative.

"If he wasn't there to catch you . . ." Ash begins.

"It's a miracle you didn't break every tooth in your mouth," Ash says. "All those years of orthodontics. . . ."

I run my tongue along my teeth. Yeah, they're all there. The rightness of my brain, however, will be more difficult to confirm, if only because it was in a highly questionable state well before I tried to belly flop onto the floor.

"So . . . how did this"—I point to my flat stomach—"happen?"

And then Ash and Ty go on to tell me what went down during my blackout.

I was rushed to the Emergency Birthcenter, where a team of medical professionals got all up in my lady parts and discovered the truth for themselves: I was mocked up. And also: I am a virgin.

"They don't see too many unbroken hymens these days," Ash jokes halfheartedly.

Heh. I really am the dying breed of a dying breed.

Faced with this indisputable physical evidence, my parents could only assume that everything else I had told them was also true. They told the doctors what I had said about the removal serum, which was retrieved from the detention center as quickly as possible.

The contents of that bottle were applied to the Billion Dollar Belly.

And then my parents and the Birthcenter staff watched—in fascination and revulsion—as my thirty-five-week-old twins simply . . . faded . . . away. . . .

"We always knew you'd rebel," Ty says. "We even factored your inevitable rebellion into our calculations and made the appropriate deductions from your total worth. But we always figured that you'd maybe rebel by getting a tattoo or chopping off all your hair."

"Like Harmony!" Ash chimes in.

"Right. Like Harmony," Ty says.

"Where is Harmony?" I ask. "Is she still here?"

Both parents ignore me. "Anyway, we figured the very worst you would do is engage in nonprocreative sexual exploration with that friend of yours. Zen."

"Zen and I never did," I add quickly. "Where is he? And Harmony?"

"I never thought I'd say this, but maybe you should have," Ash says, still avoiding my questions. "Maybe a little harmless everythingbutting would have taken the edge off and you wouldn't be in the predicament you're in right now."

My parents are beyond unbelievable. They reminded me every single day since I was fourteen years old that I had a seven-figure wager riding on my virginity. And now *I'm* the one to blame for my blinky attitude about getting physical?

"Where *is* Zen right now?" I repeat, getting more desperate by the second. "And Harmony?"

Ash and Ty reply with shrugs. Their indifference about my best friend's and sister's whereabouts would be infuriating if it weren't so totally predictable.

"We should have factored in that for someone as exceptional as you are, your youthful rebellion would be equally off the charts," Ash says, retaining control over the direction of the conversation. "And we must say, Melody, this scam of yours will go down in history as one of the scammiest ever."

When Ash says it like that, it's almost like she's *proud* of me.

"So it's our fault. All of this," Ty says. "Your fragile young mind couldn't withstand all the pressure we put on you to maximize your full potential as a Surrogette. We should have seen it coming and we should have had emergency protocols in place to stop it."

"You can bet that we've already started developing a new BestEgg seminar on this very subject," Ash says.

And that's when I delete myself from the conversation.

This is the closest my parents will get to a sincere apology. They've run my life like a corporation because—for whatever peculiar combination of nature and nurture made them the way they are—that's the only way they knew how. I have to believe that they did what they did because they loved me, and truly believed their way was the best way for me to fulfill my potential.

"Everyone loves a back-from-rock-bottom redemption story."

"It humanizes you."

"You can rehabilitate your damaged brand."

I could get upset that this experience hasn't brought us to a whole new level of compassion and understanding. But Ash and Ty are who they are. They aren't going to change now.

Fortunately for me, I'm still evolving into the person I'm supposed to be. And though they don't know it yet, and may not come to accept it, I'm done living by their protocols or anyone else's.

I'm the only one who will take credit for my successes.

And I'm the only one who will take the blame for my mistakes.

From now on, I live for me.

harmony
melody

OH MY GRACE. JONDOE DID *NOT* JUST SAY WHAT I HEARD HIM SAY.

"I really think I—I mean, *we*, can do this, Harmony," Jondoe says.

"Do *what* exactly?"

"Be a family, Harmony." He sits up straighter. "I'm ready to man up."

"Wait! Are you doing this for me? Because you think that's what *I* want?"

Jondoe looks at me quizzically. "*Isn't* that what you want?"

"No!" I protest. "That's not what I want at all!"

"Easy," Jondoe warns, placing both hands on my shoulders. "You were just glued back together a few hours ago. You don't want to burst open."

That's exactly how I feel right now. Like I'm bursting wide open! All the secrets and fears and questions I've swallowed, I've choked, I've stuffed down deep inside me for all these years are finally being released in one rapturous eruption of truth.

"I thought she would have come for them by now," I confess.

"Who?" Jondoe asks, still holding on to me. "Your sister?"

"No," I reply. "My mother."

melody
harmony

MY PARENTS ARE STILL TOO BUSY ORCHESTRATING MY COME-
back to tell me anything about Harmony and Zen when
the door opens. Lib overeagerly shoulders his way past
the security guards . . . with the Jaydens trailing closely
behind.

I don't even have time to brace myself before Lib goes
full-volume hissy pissy on me.

"HOW COULD YOU DO THIS TO ME?"

My parents immediately and literally leap to my
defense.

"Don't yell at our daughter!" Ty says, squaring his
shoulders. "This was *your* business deal gone bad!"

Ash thrusts a formidable finger in Lib's face. You've
never seen anyone point a finger like my mother.

"Just because *you* couldn't manage your own trans-actions!"

Lib turns purple. "This isn't just about business!"

And then he surprises all of us by collapsing into the nearest chair. My parents and I look at him helplessly, then at each other, then at the Jaydens.

Awkward.

I've never seen my parents so utterly stripped of hubris. It makes me like the Jaydens even more than I did when I first met them.

"We'd like to talk to your daughter alone," says the Mrs. "If you don't mind. . . ."

My parents can't resist the plaintive sadness in her voice. They are also looking for any excuse to get the hell out of this room.

"Of course," Ty says.

"If it's fine with Melody," Ash says.

I nod that it's okay.

The Birthcenter security team has crowded into the room to medicate Lib and take him elsewhere. My parents follow behind them, looking over their shoulders to make sure I'm strong enough to face what I've got coming to me. Though they are not the introspective types at all, they're probably second-guessing themselves. *Did we hire the right positive energist to train Melody for such an emotion-ally fraught confrontation?* They'll probably spend the rest of their careers trying to pinpoint the moment my file went wrong—the single flaw that caused the whole system to break down.

They may never get it: I'm not a file. I'm flawed. I'm human. My mistakes just happen to be more epically unforgivable than others.

The Mrs. looks pale and drawn, like she's aged about a decade overnight. As she approaches me, I can't help but notice that her eyes are fixated on my flattened belly.

"It's true, then?" she says in a quavering voice. "They weren't real? There aren't any babies?"

I nod solemnly, unable to speak. Her eyes skitter over my face, then settle on her husband, who is resting his hands on her waist, as if he's physically propping her up.

"We should never have listened to Lib." She says it like she means it. "We knew in our hearts this was wrong."

"He was just doing his job, you know, to talk me up," I say. "If he thought for one second that I would renegg, he would have encouraged you to go with another girl. He had no idea that I was capable of something like this."

How could he? When I didn't know it about myself?

"It's doubtful," the Mrs. says. "You look almost exactly like I did when I was your age. Lib had traveled all over the world and had never in all his years in the business seen anything like it. A 'flawless replication' he'd say."

He was for seriously wrong about the "flawless" part, wasn't he?

"He told us that you were a once-in-a-lifetime opportunity for us. You know Lib, he knows how to sell. It's what he does. And don't get us wrong, we desperately wanted the babies—I've always dreamed of being a mother—but not like this." She slowly closes her eyes. "Not like this," she repeats softly, almost to herself.

"Lib was more determined to make this deal happen with you and Jondoe than we ever were," the Mr. says, speaking up for the first time.

"Desperate," the Mrs. says.

"Desperate how?" I ask.

Why would my deal mean any more to him than the hundreds of other Conception Contracts he's negotiated? Lib always prided himself on his impartiality.

"He was desperate to help his sister."

That fall must have affected my hearing.

"His *what*?"

"Lib is my brother."

I feel like I've belly flopped onto the floor for the second time today. We both risked everything to help our sisters. Who would have thought that Lib and I had so much in common after all?

"He could have lost his RePro Rep license for negotiating a deal for a blood relative."

"Why?" I know embarrassingly little about the Surrogetting laws.

"It's a loophole that has allowed many gays like him

to come as close to fulfilling their own parental dreams as they possibly can under the Heteronormative Parenting Protocols."

"Did Lib want to be a dad?" I ask.

The Mr. and Mrs. both laugh. "Oh no. Uncle is about as much as he can handle. But he still had to rewrite the files to remove any familial connection between us. And that's why he forbade us from having any facespace interactions until after you delivered. . . ."

That sort of explains why he went psycho at the perfume launch party last night. He didn't want there to be any reason for the deal to go awry. And with all the media in attendance, all it would have taken is one especially curious MiNetter to start investigating our files and start stirring up the truth.

"Lib was the one who was being so choosy about the Sperm," the Mr. explains. "It's in his Eurosnobby nature to do so."

The Mrs. shoots the Mr. a look. I get the impression that this is an old argument. I'll bet Mr. was offended that someone of his average looks and abundant ear hair was not deemed good enough for Lib's sister.

"Lib wanted what he thought was best for us," the Mrs. says in defense of her brother. "Though truthfully, we would have been happy with any baby from any country, as long as she—"

"Or he!" chimes in the Mr.

"Or *he*, was healthy."

Her eyes flit down to my stomach once more. I nervously pull at the sheets.

"Well," I say with false cheer, "everyone hates me right now and loves and sympathizes with you. I bet Lib is fielding offers from triple-platinum Surrogettes from all over the world. You'll find someone even more up-market than I am."

The Mr. and Mrs. are both shaking their heads vigorously.

"That's out of the question," the Mr. says.

"Call us grampy and analog, but we were never comfortable with this arrangement," says the Mrs. "The idea of paying you to make a . . ."

"A couture conception!" the Mr. says mockingly. "That's what Lib always called it."

"But Lib made it seem like it was so normal . . ." the Mrs. says, losing, then regaining her focus. "He made it sound like a couple with our resources and connections would be foolish not to go for the best and the brightest baby we could afford. And we bought into it."

"In every meaning of the word," the Mr. adds with an unmistakably melancholic air.

"But this whole mess has only reinforced what we knew was wrong in our hearts all along."

"Why are you being so nice to me?" I ask. "Because if I were you, I would hate me."

"We believe in forgiveness," the Mrs. says.

252

"Forgive and be forgiven," the Mr. adds.

"Besides, *you* are not the problem," the Mrs. says, her face hardening.

And then a voice from the other side of the room says, "This whole teen pregnancy industrial complex is the problem!"

Zen!

harmony
melody

I CAN TELL FROM THE LOOK OF PITY ON HIS FACE THAT JONDOE
knows exactly which mother I'm talking about.

"I thought for sure that my birthmother would come
for me," I say, "for *us*. I thought she might want another
chance to have a family. . . ."

The heaviness of Jondoe's judgment makes it difficult
for me to continue.

"You thought your birthmom would come back to be
a mother to *your* twins?" he asks incredulously. "Like a
do-over?"

I press my trembling lips together, too embarrassed by
my own childish notions to speak. All this time I believed
my birthmother could reclaim me, and take care of me by
taking care of my babies while I tried to figure out what

kind of person I want to be.

"Oh, Harmony," is all Jondoe can say.

"I saw her, Jondoe. I had a vision of my mother. . . ." I say in a whimper.

Jondoe draws a breath and looks to the ceiling like he's consulting God directly for advice. When he lowers his head, he looks me in the eyes, though I can see that he is struggling do to so.

"It's not going to happen, Harmony," he says in a gentle but firm voice. "Your mother is not coming back for you."

"Miracles do happen!" I say with false cheer. "Not just in the Bible."

He takes my hands in his and levels me with such a grave look that I have no choice but to silence myself.

"Your mother is never coming back for you or your babies," Jondoe says, "because she is dead."

melody
harmony

ZEN RUSHES PAST THE JAYDENS. AND WITHOUT ANOTHER word, he cradles my bruised head in his hands, presses his mouth to mine, and I . . .

Dissolve.

My problems are far from over. I've destroyed the dreams of two innocent people and defrauded countless others. I've ruined my reputation, trashed my flawless file, and will surely be rejected outright by every institution of higher learning I apply to. I will be immortalized on the MiNet as the scammiest scammer in history.

But when I'm kissing Zen and he's kissing me, all the weight crushing down on me for the past eight months is finally, *finally* lifted.

We break apart reluctantly, if only because we're aware of the four eyes watching us.

"I'm Zen." He shakes the Mr.'s hand. "I don't know what Melody has told you, but I'm here to accept my share of the responsibility for what happened." His voice cracks with emotion. "I was too focused on protesting against the culture of reproductive profiteering that I never once considered that you were real people with real feelings. It was so much easier to scam you when you were anonymous cradlegrabbers. . . ." Zen covers his mouth. "No offense!"

Immediately the Mrs. and Mr. start shaking their heads in protest.

"You and Melody exercised poor judgment, yes," says the Mrs. "But *we're* the adults here. *We're* the ones who participated in and therefore perpetuated the culture of . . . what did you say?"

"Which part? Reproductive profiteering? The teen pregnancy industrial complex?" Zen provides helpfully.

"All of it." The Mrs. takes her husband's hand in hers. "That's why we're going to drop all charges against you, and hope that any aspiring litigants do the same."

I shake my head in disbelief.

"Make no mistake, what you did was . . ." She swallows loudly. "*Wrong.* But we are *all* part of the problem here. And the locus of blame cannot and should not fall on two teenagers."

I'm for seriously about to cry. At this point, I'm beyond wishing that the Jaydens fulfill their dream of becoming parents. I want them to be *my* parents.

"That's what we're going to tell the world." She stops to look at me meaningfully. "Whenever you're ready."

"Really?" I ask, still not believing what I'm hearing.

"Really," says the Mrs. "You two obviously have a lot to catch up on first. So we'll leave you alone for a few moments while we prepare our statement. I have to warn you, though. The media isn't going to hold off for too much longer."

The Mr. and Mrs. leave the room and close the door behind them.

Zen and I lock eyes.

And before I even know what's happening, our hands and mouths are all over each other again. . . .

But this isn't the time or place.

FOR SERIOUS, MELODY. THIS ISN'T THE TIME OR PLACE TO GET ALL HUMPY.

I literally have to push him off me or I would never stop kissing and being kissed. Can you blame me? I'm running on almost seventeen years' worth of pent-up lust. . . .

And love?

"So you forgive me?" Zen says breathlessly.

I playfully tug on his hair spikes.

"If the Jaydens can forgive me, I can forgive you," I say. "I can forgive Ventura. I can forgive my parents. I can forgive Lib. I can forgive anyone."

I can only hope that the world feels the same way about me.

And if it doesn't, then I guess I deserve whatever I've got coming to me.

harmony

melody

I FEEL LIKE I'VE BEEN KICKED IN THE CHEST.

"She's not dead," I gasp. "You're just saying that so I don't get my hopes up. . . ."

"No, I'm not," Jondoe says somberly. "And I'm sorry to tell you that she is."

"You've lied to me before!" I rail, pushing him away from me. "You're lying to me right now to get what you want."

"What I want," Jondoe says, "is for you to be happy. And for me to be happy. And in the best scenario, for us to be happy together. You have every right to be suspect of everything I say. I would respect you less if you didn't mistrust me a little, because I've got a disreputable past.

But I would never lie about something like this, Harmony. Especially when I wanted so much for the opposite to be true for you. That's why I pushed so hard for Lib to tell me the truth."

"Lib?" I ask. "Lib knew?"

Jondoe nods. "As your representative it's his job to know the unknowable. That's what makes him the best, right?" He sighs heavily. "He's been trying to track Melody's—and your—birthmother since he signed your sister almost four years ago. I guess her DNA came up in the death databank sometime in the past year."

"What do you know about her? Was she young? Was she a musician? Did she—"

Jondoe cuts me off. "Lib wouldn't tell me anything other than that she's dead. I don't know if he knows any more than that."

"How long have you known the truth?"

"Since your first trimester."

"Why didn't you tell me?"

"I would have if you had been willing to talk to me. I almost confessed to Melody, but when she told me how desperate you were to meet your birthmother, I just couldn't crush your hopes like that. If I had any idea what you were really thinking, about creating a new family." He lowers his head. "I'm sorry."

My birthmother is dead. I'll never meet her. She'll never answer my questions. She'll never help me.

261

"Your father is still out there somewhere but . . ."

"But he might not even know he's a father," I finish for him.

He nods solemnly.

I feel hollowed out. Too empty to cry.

"Melody doesn't know?"

"I don't think so," Jondoe says. "Not unless Lib told her."

I need my sister. She was never as invested in finding our birthmother as I was, but she deserves to hear the truth.

"Where is Mel?"

I don't know if he was listening in or not, but right at that moment, Ram rushes into the room.

"They've dropped all charges against her!" Ram announces.

"Melody?"

"Yes! She's on the MiVu right now!"

And before he's finished saying it, Melody comes forward, larger than life on the wall. She's wearing a light green hospital gown that hangs loosely from her trim frame, exactly like the one I'm wearing right now. . . .

"Wait a moment! Is that the Birthcenter in the background? Is she *here*? Why didn't you tell me she was here?"

"She's on another floor," Ram explains. "Her parents brought her in when she jumped off a table at the detention center."

"She *what*?" Jondoe and I ask at the same time.

"They thought she, um, tried to, you know," Ram mumbles, "*end* those babies—"

"But she wasn't even pregnant!" Jondoe interjects.

"Her parents didn't know that at the time," Ram explains. "But they know now."

Sure enough, Ash and Ty come forward and flank Melody on either side. I hope that they are actually being supportive of their only daughter and aren't just taking advantage of this international attention.

"When I betrayed my brand, I betrayed America," Melody is saying in a quavery voice. "So I, um . . . want to apologize to everyone who believed in The Hotties, believed in me."

She stops midsentence and nervously glances over her shoulder at someone out of the scope of the lens. Draws in a breath. Purses her lips in concentration. Then her eyes light up from within, like she's just touched the matchstick to the wick.

"Our whole world has gone"—she hesitates slightly— "*baby* crazy." You can practically hear the collective intake of breath. "That's right. I said the B-word. And I'll say it again. Baby! Baby! Baby!" She's smiling now, getting braver. "That's what we're dealing with here. Not *bumps* or *preggs* or *deliveries*," she says each word pointedly. "Or whatever other euphemism you want to use to distance yourself from the truth. We're making babies. We're creating *people*. And we're having meaningless sex to do it! And yet we pretend like it's no big deal. We pretend that we aren't in the business of buying and selling *human beings. . . .*"

At this point I see Ty tightening his grip on Melody's arm.

"I think we're done here!" Ash sing-songs.

"No!" Melody tells her. "I'm not done yet." She shakes off her dad's arm and takes another step forward, closer to the cameras. "I know that there are girls who have been put in far worse situations than me. These are the girls we don't want to talk about, the ones who have been kidnapped—"

"This isn't polite talk!" exclaims Ash.

"Isn't polite?" Melody asks incredulously. "Isn't *polite*? I'm not farting at the dinner table! I'm talking about baby trafficking! That's beyond impolite. It's inhumane! And it's tough to talk about. But it's happening right nowwww."

"Shut these cameras off!" Ty menaces, but the media ignores him. They know this is history in the making.

Melody does too. She continues calmly and confidently.

"I bet what I'm saying makes a lot of sense to you girls out there. How many of you have felt the pressure to pregg? How many of you have bumped with someone you barely know? Or have put off getting physical with someone you really, really care about and, um . . ." When she glances off camera again, her cheeks flush pink. "Maybe even love . . ."

"She's talking about Zen!" Ram says giddily.

264

"Shhhhh!"

"But you can't be with him because he doesn't meet the minimum Standards, or because you're contracted to bump with someone you don't care about at all! We've got it all backwards! We should be able to bond emotionally and physically—not either/or. And if you're an amateur lucky enough to be with someone you love or like *a lot* or—at the very least—*genuinely* lust after without the artificial humpiness of Tocin or some other off-brand drug, why does it always have to end in the delivery room? Shouldn't we be able to have sex without making babies? Condoms are legal in other countries, like Sweden and Norway, and the birthrates aren't falling any more drastically than our own. . . ."

There's some booing. And an angry voice in the crowd shouts, "Socialist!" Ty is literally grabbing at Melody's hand to try to drag her off camera, but she is unbowed.

"I'm obviously striking a nerve here. But if my stunt makes you all think a little bit more about the pressure our government, our media, our schools, our *parents*"—she shoots a look at Ash and Ty—"are putting on us—we're carrying the weight and *fate* of Western civilization, for Darwin's sake!—then I don't regret doing it. I'm just sorry that in taking a stand, I stomped on someone else's dreams."

There's a moment's pause, followed by the faint sound of one person clapping, soon joined by another set of hands. The sound gets louder as the applauders approach Melody from behind, on the opposite side of her parents. One is a man I've never seen before and the other . . .

I don't believe my eyes.

It can't be.

"Harmony? What's wrong?" Jondoe asks.

"You look like you've seen a ghost," Ram adds.

"I have! I mean, I am! That's *her*!"

"Who?" Jondoe asks.

"My birthmother! She *is* alive! And she found us!"

Ram freezes, petrified. Jondoe looks at me, then the wall, then back at me.

"The blond woman behind Melody! She's the one I saw in the sky! It's her! I'm certain of it! You were wrong! Lib was wrong! My birthmother lives! Miracles *do* happen!"

I know I sound crazy. But she is the same woman I saw in my dream, welcoming me into Heaven.

Jondoe approaches me cautiously, with Ram following close behind.

"That's *not* your birthmother, Harmony."

Jondoe doesn't know what he's talking about. She's the spitting image of me and Melody! Or we're the spitting image of her! She's beautiful, and I hope I don't sound immodest when I say that because I look just like her, but she is. The twins will be blessed to grow up to look like her too.

The camera zooms in on her radiant face as she starts speaking.

"Turn it up! I have to hear what she has to say!" I've waited my whole life for this. Tears spring to my eyes at the very notion of hearing her, my birthmother, say my name aloud.

"Harmony!" Jondoe snaps his fingers in front of my eyes. "I know you want to believe she's your birthmother. But she's not . . ."

But I'm not listening to him. I'm ready to listen to her when she speaks directly to the millions of eyes watching, confident and unafraid. I'm going to hear my birthmother's voice for the very first time. Was Melody right about her ambitions? Will she have a musical voice?

"I want everyone to know that my husband and I have forgiven Melody Mayflower for her deception, and the world should forgive her too." She smiles at Melody, but it's a joyless smile. "Melody isn't to blame here. We are to blame. She is a product—and I mean that in both senses of the word—of her times. We need to look at ourselves, and the conception-crazy culture we have created that have turned girls in breeding machines." She inhales and holds her head up high. "That is all."

Her face is just starting to crumple when she turns and buries her face into the shoulder of a man I don't recognize. He is also crying.

And now I'm crying too.

This isn't the reunion I've been longing for.

My birthmother hasn't found me.

And if she hasn't by now . . .

"I tried telling you, Harmony," Jondoe says, patting my hair soothingly.

She never will. Jondoe was telling the truth. She's dead.

"Who is she then?" I eke out.

"The Mrs. who hired Melody and me."

I take a long shuddery breath as I let this sink in.

I *know* she's the woman I saw in my dream, even if it doesn't make any logical sense. I refuse to believe that my God-given vision was a meaningless hallucination. There is a reason why all of this is happening. But I hope the Lord doesn't get offended if I can't just sit idly and wait for that reason to present itself on its own.

"I need to see my sister," I say.

Ram hops up and takes off toward the door.

"And tell Melody I want to meet her."

"Meet who?" Ram and Jondoe ask.

"The Mrs.," I reply.

Jondoe waits until Ram leaves the room before placing a comforting hand on my knee. "But she's not your birthmother. . . ."

"I know that," I say, giving him a fragile smile.

What I don't say is that I believe our meeting holds a greater purpose.

melody
harmony

EVEN THOUGH I'VE ALREADY GIVEN THE MINET ENOUGH
material to last a millennium—my optics must be going
off the spring right now—no one interferes when Ram
picks me up, throws me over his shoulder, and carries me
through the crowd and into the hospital. It's all great material. The paparazzi and reporters must sense I'm going to
drop out of eyesight when this day is over, so they better
capture glimpses of me while they still can.

"Thanks, Ram," I say when he sets me down outside
Harmony's room. "What you did today was very brave."

"You too," he replies.

"I hope you and Zeke can be happy together now
that you aren't living a lie." He presses his hands together

like he's praying, kisses his steepled fingertips, and blows it in my direction.

"You too."

I put my hand on the doorknob. "Are you coming in?"

"No," he replies. "Now I have to get the Mrs."

And he takes off before I can ask why.

When I open the door to see Harmony sitting up in the hospital bed, I'm flooded with relief. She's still here.

"Melody!"

"Harmony!"

I'm afraid if I hug her too tightly I'll bust her belly glue. She has no such reservations and squeezes me flat against her.

I pull away so I can get a good look at her.

"Your hair!"

She touches her bangs as if she'd forgotten all about cutting and coloring her hair.

"Just when I've sort of gotten used to someone looking exactly like me, you don't look anything like me anymore," I say with a laugh. "Are you okay?"

"Are *you* okay?" she asks, always thinking of others before herself.

"Well, the name Melody Mayflower will forever be synonymous with the biggest case of procreative malfeasance in history—"

I stop myself midsentence. There's so much to talk about, and quite honestly, my legal troubles are the least pressing of my concerns. My sister had two babies! She is responsible for the welfare for two new human beings who didn't exist this morning.

Is she responsible?

"So . . . Harmony . . ." I begin cautiously. "The twins . . ."

Harmony pats the bed, encouraging me to slide in beside her. She rests her head on my shoulder, sighs.

"Our birthmother is dead."

This wasn't what I was expecting her to say. And yet the news of her death doesn't come as a shock to me. I think I've always known that we would never meet. Still, I'm saddened by the news. Not just for Harmony, who always longed for a reunion more than I did, but for me. It would have been nice to meet my biomom, to see if I get my rebellious streak from her, or if it was the natural consequence of being raised by such controlling parents.

Parents who meant well. But . . .

"I thought she might come for the babies," Harmony continues.

"Who? Our biomom?"

Harmony nods. "I thought she might want to make up for giving us up . . ."

"Ohhhh . . ." is all I can say as the truth dawns on me, why she wasn't at all prepared for the twins' arrival. Harmony has been brought up to believe in redemption stories. She truly believed that her—our—biomom would come back to redeem herself. She'd get a second chance with Harmony's twins to make up for the twins she left behind almost seventeen years ago.

For this scenario to unfold, it would have required our biomom to regret what she did in the first place. Maybe she never had any reason to regret leaving us on the doorstep of Princeton Medical Center nearly seventeen years ago. Maybe she went on to live a rich and rewarding life, a life she would never have lived if she had kept us. Or maybe she led a punishing life, one that would have been even more difficult if she had two babies to care for. A life she wouldn't want to wish on anyone else, especially her own flesh and blood.

This is why I've tried not to think about my biomom. Such speculation only leads to mystery (at best) or misery (at worst). Neither of which are particularly satisfying outcomes.

"Your idea really wasn't so crazy," I tell her. "If the Virus isn't cured, Americans will eventually adapt with the rest of the world. We'll still have babies young, but our parents—the grandparents, or even great-grandparents—will raise the babies while we grow up ourselves. Then when our own children have babies, that's when *we'll* step up."

Harmony nods like this all makes perfect sense, which it should, because the concept of shared parenting isn't so different from how it works in Goodside—only without the enforced marriage and end of education at age thirteen.

"You—*we*—are just a generation too early. All these

twenty- and thirtysomethings like the Jaydens still remember the way it used to be and want it that way," I say. "We're the ones that will have to make the change."

I've been told my whole life that I've got all the power. But it's only now that I'm beginning to believe it. My days of selling junk food and perfume are over. If the world is going to listen to me, I better start saying things that are worth hearing. The problem is, our paradigm-shifting potential does Harmony no good in the right here and now. I'm trying to figure out how to broach the subject of what will happen with her twins when Harmony speaks up.

"I want to meet the Jaydens," Harmony says matter-of-factly. "I think they're the parents for my twins."

Oh no. Zen had long ago warned me that Harmony might feel guilted into giving up her babies.

"Oh, Harmony!" I say, clutching her hands. "You don't have to do this for me. . . ."

"I'm not doing it for you," Harmony says. "I'm doing it for the twins. I'm doing it for the Jaydens. I'm doing it for *me*."

How can she even think about giving up the twins when our abandonment by our birthmother has been such a source of torment? And she never took a single dose of Anti-Tocin. What if she *bonded* with those babies?

"Have you seen them?"

"Yes," she says. "And that's when I made my final

decision. They deserve so much better than me."

"But you'll make a great mother!" I argue. "And Jondoe is ready to man up. He's only told me so like, every day for the past eight and a half months."

"He only said that because that's what he thought I wanted. But we're not ready to be parents," she says, shaking her head. "And after hearing what the Jaydens said, and seeing their capacity for forgiveness, I know that they will be better parents to these babies than I can be right now. How can I possibly raise two daughters when I don't know anything about the world? Or myself?"

I can see the fiery determination in her eyes, hear the conviction in her voice.

"There are so many things I've never done," she says. "That's why I need to leave, Melody. It's time to stop pretending that only the Elders' interpretations of the Bible will lead to grace. There's more to life than a book that was written thousands of years ago by a bunch of men who couldn't even agree amongst themselves."

"Don't feel bad about what you haven't done. Experience isn't everything," I say, thinking about all the accomplishments in my file. "I've done a lot of things and I'm not exactly fulfilled."

"But how much of your life was your choice?" she asks pointedly. "I was as beholden to the Bible as you were to your Surrogette file."

Valid point.

"Being with Jondoe was really the first decision I made all on my own. And despite what's happened since, I don't regret my choice."

"Well, that's *one* thing you've done that I haven't," I say, my voice trailing off mischievously.

Harmony blushes crimson and playfully swats my arm. "Melody!"

"I'm merely pointing out that you are way ahead of me in at least one area of expertise. . . ."

And we both laugh our snorty laughs. When I first met Harmony, I couldn't imagine making such a joke in front of her. I certainly couldn't picture her laughing about it. It makes me excited to think about how much more we can learn about each other now that we can finally be ourselves. What a world of wonders awaits her! I want to share the best of everything on this side of the gates.

"I can't wait to introduce you—"

She cuts in. "I *want* you to introduce me!"

"Um," I say, not knowing where to start. "I wasn't expecting your pop cultural tutorial to begin right this second."

Harmony shakes her head. "I'm talking about the Jaydens. I want to meet the parents of my twins."

Harmony is not letting go of this. She's more certain of this than any decision she's ever made in her life.

Not that she's had the opportunity to make that many decisions.

"Please, Melody," she pleads.

"Okay," I say, before making my way out to the hall. "I'll introduce you."

I don't know if she's making the right choice, but it's not my choice to make. I promise to support her, whatever she decides.

Because that's what sisters do.

harmony
melody

JONDOE OPENS THE DOOR AND PEEKS HIS HEAD INSIDE.

"Are you *sure* this is what you want?"

"I'm sure," I reply.

He nods resolutely. "Then this is what I want too."

He holds the door open all the way, welcoming the Jaydens into the room with a sweep of his free hand.

"Harmony, the Jaydens," he says cordially. "The Jaydens, Harmony."

The first thing I notice is that the Mrs. is not the same woman I saw in my dream. That woman was a figment of my imagination. The hallucinogenic product of the anesthesia.

This woman, and this man, are real.

And I believe they are the parents of the twins.

melody
harmony

A NURSE IS WAITING FOR ME IN THE HALL.

"A handsome young man asked me to give you this," she says, handing over a piece of paper with a smile and a wink.

WAITING 4 U. ROOF. IGNORE THE SIGN.

"Where are my parents?" I ask her.

"They're fielding media inquiries, I think," she says. "You should follow your friend. I don't know how much longer I can safeguard your privacy."

I take the elevator all the way up to the top. I'm surprised when it opens up to a glassed-in rooftop garden. I wouldn't have thought that an Emergency Birthcenter would even bother with such an amenity when its goal is to get patients in and out as quickly as possible. It's winter, so most of the plants are leafless, flowerless, but I imagine that it would be lush and welcoming come spring. And though it's not as cold in here as it is outside, I shiver when my bare foot touches the bluestone walkway. My hospital gown doesn't provide much warmth.

There's a low fence blocking the entrance, with a sign saying:

THE ZORAH HARDING FERTILITY TERRARIUM IS TEMPO-RARILY CLOSED. THANK YOU FOR NOT TRESPASSING.

I climb over the barricade and see Zen posing trium-phantly on top of a stone bench.

"What a speech!" Zen says. "Far more powerful than any Contra/Ception slogan I could have come up with."

"I wasn't saying it for the Mission."

He hops off the bench and lands right in front of me. He chivalrously removes his insulated jacket and puts it around my shoulders. Then he leans in to kiss me again, and as much as I want to kiss him back, I have to say some-thing first.

"I wasn't saying it for you, either," I say, pressing my hand against his chest. I can feel his heart beating even faster than my own. He wants me as much as I want him, but there are certain things that cannot be left unsaid. "I was saying it for me. I was saying it for Harmony. And for all the girls out there who have ever felt like bumping was the only way to make something of ourselves."

He relaxes out of his lunge for my lips.

"And you succeeded, Mel! You've started a movement. You're more famous than ever before."

"Infamous, maybe," I say.

"Legendary!" He's hopping up and down he's so amped. "Have you read any of your MiNet messages?"

I blanch at the thought of it.

"You're a hero, Melody! Millions of girls from all over the world are thanking you for saying what you said!"

"Wh—?"

"And, yes, there are millions more who think you should rot in jail," he says quickly, "but that's not important right now."

This is too much. I have to sit down.

"You're not going to believe this. Zorah Harding came forward and confessed that she faked her last four pregnancies!"

The Zorah Harding, the namesake of this fertility garden, who delivered ten babies in seven years? The most prolific breeder since the Virus was discovered?

Zen nods, as if he's reading my thoughts.

"The same! She was pressured into getting mocked up because she's a procreative role model for all American girls to look up to! The Save America Society and the National Association for Procreation were totally in on it! It's a huuuuuge scandal, Mel! They are all in way more trouble than you are!"

My mind is blown. I'm not the biggest scammer in the

history of scams after all. With my parents' obsession with me being number one, I can't help but wonder if this news will come as a sort of a disappointment to them.

"How are my parents taking all this?" I ask.

"Are you kidding? They're thrilled! They're making more media than ever before! They're already taking credit for your transformation from traitor to whistle-blowing righter of wrongs."

Of course they are. I have to remind myself again: My parents are who they are. I can't change them. I can only change myself.

"And you haven't heard the best of it, Mel," Zen says. "Do you realize how many American teens had no idea that condoms were legal in other countries?"

"*I* had no idea until you told me," I say, wincing with embarrassment.

"There's already a spike in the international Free Love tourism industry," Zen says. "We've been offered an all-expenses–paid trip to Oslo."

"Oh no," I say. "No more branding for me. I'm retired."

"Are you suuuuure?" he says, wiggling his eyebrows with mock lustiness.

"I'm sure," I say. "If we take a trip to Norway for some free love, it's going to be on *my* terms."

"Okay," he says, holding up his palms in surrender. "But just remember that there's no shortage of potential sponsors who DO NOT want us to procreate. . . ."

I smile weakly and Zen immediately senses that something is wrong.

"What is it?" he asks, sitting back down beside me on the bench.

"Does it ever make you sad?" I ask.

"Does *what* ever make me sad?"

"The idea that we won't ever have a child together," I say shyly.

"WHAT?!" He reels back in shock. "Melody Mayflower! You want my seed?"

"Ew! No!" And when Zen flinches, I add, "Um. No offense."

"None taken, I guess," he says. "So what are you getting at?"

"I just wonder if, like, when I'm older, like the Jaydens' age, I'll regret not doing it when I still could," I say. "That's an honest question to ask myself, isn't it?"

Zen nods thoughtfully.

"Can you imagine being a mother right now?"

"No."

"Can you imagine your parents helping you?"

"No," I say with a snort. "No way."

"Well, that's your answer then, isn't it?"

He takes my hand in his and holds it in such an innocent, non-humpy way that I feel like my heart is going to explode. One day I'll tell him that the saddest part about choosing not to make a baby with him is depriving the world of a human being with half his brilliant, beautiful, nerdy DNA.

And mine.

When I lean over to kiss him on the cheek, I feel the heat of his blush on my lips.

One day I'll tell him.

But not today.

harmony
melody

WE'RE IN THE NURSERY NOW. THE GIRLS ARE AWAKE, KICKING their tiny feet and punching their little fists in the air. It's hard to believe that until a few hours ago, they were kicking and punching inside me.

The Jaydens are rocking back and forth on their heels in anticipation.

"Do you want to hold them?"

"Yes!" the Mr. and Mrs. reply with such unbridled enthusiasm that we all can't help but laugh.

They gaze upon these girls with awe and wonder and humility. The Jaydens know that these girls are precious blessings.

"Do you have names picked out?" Jondoe asks.

The Jaydens glance nervously at each other, afraid to look presumptuous.

I try to reassure them. "I'd like to hear them," I say encouragingly.

"Faith," says the Mrs. holding up one girl in her arms.

"Mercy," says the Mr. holding up the other girl in his arms.

Hearing the girls called by their names for the first time brings joyous tears to all of our eyes. It's a beautiful moment, and right now I feel more in touch with a higher power than I ever did in prayerclique. I feel connected to the Jaydens in a spiritual, even miraculous way, so much so that I just have to ask.

"Do you have God?"

"Yes." The Mrs. answers. "We believe."

And the Mr. adds with a smile, "Now more than ever before."

Me too.

I have no intention on ever returning to Goodside, but now I'm confident that I don't have to. The Jaydens have shown me that I can pursue faith on this side of the gates as well as—or even better—than I ever did before. Just in a different way.

"We don't want to pressure you, but it's our hope that you can be a part of their lives," the Mrs. says. "We want our daughters to know both of you. In whatever capacity feels right for you."

This is more than I could ever ask for. I was so afraid that they might not ever let me see them again. As much as I knew such restrictions would pain me, I was even more afraid of the effects my absence could have on them. I didn't want them to suffer as I have with uncertainty. Now they would have a chance at understanding that I've chosen this path not because they were unloved, but because they were loved so much.

The Jaydens are looking at me eagerly, still waiting for me to respond to their proposition. But I'm so overcome with gratitude that I can only muster a teary glugging noise.

"I think what she means is yes," Jondoe says, putting his arm around me.

I don't know what is going to happen with Jondoe. I don't doubt that he wants to be with me. But he needs to learn that I'm more than just the good girl sent from Heaven to make him a better believer. I only know that I need to learn more about myself before I can possibly commit to anyone else. I hope that Jondoe will be patient with me as I discover what kind of life I'll choose to live, what kind of person I'll decide to be.

And yet, I'm grateful for this gift that the Jaydens have given us, as it guarantees that no matter what happens to us romantically, Jondoe and I too will have a bond that can never be broken.

The word bursts out of me.

"Yes!"

melody
harmony

I TAP THE NURSERY WINDOW AND GIVE HARMONY A DOUBLE thumbs-up. She and Jondoe join me and Zen in the hall to give the Jaydens time alone with their new daughters.

"I can't get over your hair," I say.

"I wanted something different," she replies.

"Well, you certainly got it!" I joke, giving her hair a playful tousle.

"I mean in life," she says. "I want to give living in Otherside a try. I want the freedom to . . ."

To what? Harmony is overwhelmed by how much she doesn't know.

"To make your own decisions?" I suggest.

"To sometimes succeed and to sometimes fail spectacularly?" Zen adds.

Jondoe searches my sister's eyes. "And start all over again?"

She holds his gaze, nods wordlessly. I put my arm around her.

"Me too."

harmony
melody

THE JAYDENS APPROACH THE GLASS AND BECKON FOR MELODY and me to come inside.

"Oh, I don't know," Melody says. "I've never actually held a baby before. . . ."

After we're sufficiently sanitized, I show Melody how to cradle her arms. The Mrs. gently places one of the infants right into the crook of her elbow.

"This is Mercy," the Mrs. says.

Melody is saucer-eyed and stiff as a board, terrified to move.

I've helped care for babies since I was barely out of diapers myself. I take Faith from the Mr. and show Melody how to relax her posture.

"Thank you," the Jaydens say before leaving us alone in the nursery.

Melody looks panicked.

"They're so helpless," she says, staring agog at Mercy's sleeping face. "They have no idea what they're in for."

I gently press my hand against the rise and fall of Faith's tiny chest. I can feel her heart pulsing against my fingertips: *thumpthumpthumpthumpthump*.

"They're stronger than you think," I say.

I pray that it will be different when they're our age.

I pray for a cure to the Virus so they can choose not to share their bodies before they're ready. I pray that they will have the power to choose when and how they will marry, make love, make babies. And I pray that they will not be judged if they choose not to do those things in the "right" order.

"*We're* stronger too," Melody replies.

My sister and I close our eyes. We dream of a better world. We imagine what we can—and will—do to make it possible.

For us.

And for the girls.

MEGAN MCCAFFERTY is the author of *Bumped* as well as the *New York Times* bestselling Jessica Darling series, which includes *Sloppy Firsts*, *Second Helpings*, *Charmed Thirds*, *Fourth Comings*, and *Perfect Fifths*. She lives in Princeton, New Jersey, with her family. You can visit Megan online at www.meganmccafferty.com.

**Society says you've got a perfect future.
But what if you wanted something else?**

Find out how Melody and Harmony's story began in this
sharp, sassy and futuristic take on teen pregnancy
– BUMPED is wildly original, totally readable
and scarily believable.